MW01025491

Journey into Christmas

BOOKS BY BESS STREETER ALDRICH
AVAILABLE IN BISON BOOK EDITIONS

The Rim of the Prairie (BB 347)
Spring Came On Forever (BB 904)
Journey into Christmas and Other Stories (BB 934)

BESS STREETER ALDRICH

Journey into Christmas

AND OTHER STORIES

Illustrations by JAMES ALDRICH

University of Nebraska Press
Lincoln and London

Copyright 1949 by Appleton-Century-Crofts, Inc.
All rights reserved
Manufactured in the United States of America

First Bison Book printing: 1985
Most recent printing indicated by the first digit below:
1   2   3   4   5   6   7   8   9   10

*All names, characters, and events in this
book are fictional, and any resemblance
which may seem to exist to real persons
is purely coincidental.*

Copyright, 1928, 1936, 1937, 1938, 1939, 1947, 1948
"Youth Is All of an Up-and-Coming" copyright 1931
by Physical Culture Magazine

Library of Congress Cataloging in Publication Data
Aldrich, Bess Streeter, 1881–1954.
Journey into Christmas and other stories.
Reprint. Originally published: New York:
Appleton-Century-Crofts, c1949.
1. Christmas stories. I. Title.
PS3501.L378J68   1985   813'.52   85-8559
ISBN 0-8032-5908-5 (pbk.)

Reprinted by arrangement with E. P. Dutton, Inc.

CONTENTS

Journey into Christmas

MARGARET STALEY stood at her library window looking out at the familiar elms and the lace-vine arbor. Tonight the trees were snow-crusted, the arbor a thing of crystal filigree under the Christmas stars.

Some years the Midwest stayed mild all through December, donning its snowsuit only after the holidays. But tonight was a Christmas Eve made to order, as though Nature had supervised the designing and decorating of a silvered stage setting.

Margaret Staley visualized all this perfection, but she knew that the very beauty of the scene brought into sharper contrast the fact that for the first time in her life she was alone on Christmas Eve.

For fifty-nine Christmases she had been surrounded by the people she loved. On this sixtieth, there was no one. For not one of her four children was coming home.

She could remember reading a story like that

once, about a mother who was disappointed that no one was coming—and then, just at dusk on Christmas Eve, all the children and their families arrived together to surprise her. But that was a sentimental piece of fiction; this was cold reality.

The reasons for none of the four coming were all good. Three of the reasons were, anyway, she admitted reluctantly. Calling the roll she went over—for the hundredth time—why each could not make the trip.

Don. That was understandable. Don and Janet, his wife, and young Ralph in California could not be expected to come half way across the continent every year, and they had been here last Christmas. She herself had visited them the past summer, returning as late as September.

Ruth. Ruth was her career daughter, connected with a children's hospital and vitally important to her post. Long ago she had accepted the fact that Ruth could give her only the fragments from a busy life and never had she begrudged it; indeed, she had felt vicariously a part of her capable daughter's service to humanity.

Jean. Jeanie and her husband, Roy, lived in Chicago. Jeanie was a great family girl and certainly would have come out home, but the two little boys were in quarantine.

Lee. The hurt which she had loyally pushed into the back of her mind jumped out again like an unwanted and willful jack-in-the-box. Lee and his Ann could have come. Living in Oklahoma, not too far away, they could have made the trip if they had wished. Or if it had not been convenient for Lee to leave, she could have gone down there to be with them. *If they had asked her.*

The only time Christmas had been mentioned was in a letter, now several weeks old. Lee had mentioned casually that they were going to have company for Christmas. That would be Ann's folks of course. You mustn't be selfish. You had to remember that there were in-laws to be taken into consideration.

Standing there at the window, looking out at the silver night, she remembered how she once thought the family would always come home. In her younger years she had said complacently, "I know my children. They love their old home and whenever possible they will spend Christmas in it. Of course there will be sickness and other reasons to keep them away at times, but some of the four will always be here." And surprisingly it had been true. Someone had been here every Christmas.

Faintly into her reveries came the far-off sound of bells and she opened the casement window a bit to locate their tinkling. It was the carolers, carrying out the town's traditional singing on Christmas Eve.

She closed the window and drew the drapes, as though unable to bear the night's white beauty and the poignant notes of young voices.

"I'm alone ... I'm alone ... it's Christmas Eve and I'm alone." Her mind repeated it like some mournful raven with its "nevermore."

Suddenly she caught herself by a figurative grip. "Now, listen," she said to that self which was grieving. "You are not a weak person and you're not neurotic. You have good sense and understanding and even humor at times. How often have you criticized people for this very thing?"

She walked over to the radio and turned it on, but when *"Silent Night ... Holy Night"* came softly forth, she snapped it off, afraid she would break down and weep like an old Niobe.

"Oh, go on ... feel sorry for yourself if you want to. Go on. Do it." She smiled again wryly, and knew she was trying to clutch at humor, that straw which more than once had saved her from drowning in troubled waters.

She went over to her desk and got out the four last letters from the children, although she knew their contents thoroughly.

There was the fat one from Don and Janet with young Ralph's hastily scribbled sixth-grade enclosure. They said the poinsettias were up to the back porch roof, that the Christmas parade had been spectacular, and that they would all be thinking of her on Christmas day when they drove to Laguna Beach.

Then the letter from Jeanie. She had been experiencing one of those times which mothers have to expect, but they were over the hump now and although still in quarantine, she thought Bud could be dressed and Larry sit up by Christmas day. They would all miss the annual trip out home but would be thinking of her.

Ruth's letter was a series of disconnected notes written in odd moments at her desk. Almost one could catch a whiff of hospital odors from them. They were filled with plans for the nurses, the carols, the trees for the convalescents, but as always she would think, too, of home and mother on Christmas day.

From Lee and Ann, nothing but that three-, no, *four*-weeks-old letter with its single casual reference to Christmas. There was a package from them under the tree, attractively packed and addressed in Ann's handwriting. It, too, had been here for weeks. But no recent letter. No special. No wire. No "We will be thinking of you" as the others had written. She tried to push the hurt back and close the lid on it, but she could not forget it was there.

She put the letters away and went into the living room. It looked as big as Grand Central Station. Last year there had been eleven sitting in these chairs which tonight were as empty as her heart. Half ashamed at her childishness in trying to create an illusion, she began pulling them out to form the semicircle of last year when the big tree had been its pivotal point. She could even recall where each had sat that morning at the opening of the gifts. Jeanie and Bud on the davenport, Ruth curled up on the hassock, Ann and Lee side by side in the big blue chairs—and on around the circle.

She had to smile again to remember the red rocking-chair which she brought from the storeroom for young Larry. It had been her own little rocker and was fifty-eight years old. A

brown tidy hung limply on its cane back, an old-fashioned piece worked in cross-stitch, the faded red letters reading: FOR MARGARET. Larry had squeezed into it, but when his name was called and he rose excitedly to get his first present, the chair rose with him and they had to pry him out of it and one of the chair's arms cracked. There had been so much hilarious laughter where tonight was only silence. And silence can be so very much louder than noise.

With the chairs forming their ghost-like semicircle beside her, she turned her own around to the fireplace and sat down to give herself the pleasure and the pain of remembering old Christmases. Swiftly her mind traversed the years, darting from one long gone holiday season to another.

The Christmas before Don was born she and John were in their first new home. They had been very happy that year, just the two of them; so happy in fact that she had felt almost conscience stricken to think she could be contented without her own old family at holiday time. Why, she thought suddenly, that was the way Lee was feeling now, and she could not help a twinge of jealousy at the parting of the ways.

Then Don's first Christmas when he was

eleven months old. After these thirty-six years she could still remember how he clutched a big glass marble and would not notice anything else. Strange how such small details stayed in one's mind.

The Christmas before Jeanie was born, when she did not go out to shop, but sent for her gifts by mail, so that the opening of them was almost as much a surprise to her as to the recipients.

Then there was the whooping-cough Christmas, with the house full of medicated steam and all four youngsters dancing and whooping spasmodically around the tree like so many little Indians.

There was the time she bought the big doll for Ruth and when it proved to have a large paint blemish on its leg, she wanted to return it for a perfect one. But Ruth would not hear of it and made neat little bandages for the leg as though it were a wound. It was the first she ever noticed Ruth's nursing instincts.

Dozens of memories flocked to her mind. There had not always been happy holidays. Some of them were immeasurably sad. Darkest of all was the one after John's death, with the children trying to carry out cheerfully the old family customs, knowing that it was what Dad would have wanted. But even in the troubled days there had been warm companionship to share the burden—not this icy loneliness.

For a few moments she sat, unmoving, lost in the memory of that time, then roused herself to continue her mental journeying.

Soon after that dark one, Christmas was no longer a childish affair. Gifts suddenly ceased to be skates and hockey-sticks and became sorority party dresses and fraternity rings, and the house was full of young people home for vacation. Then the first marriage and Don's Janet was added to the circle, then Jeanie brought Roy into it. In time the first grandson ... and another ... and a third—all the youthful pleasure of the older members of the family renewed through the children's eyes.

Then came that Christmas when the blast of the ships in their harbor had sent its detonations here into this very living room, as into every one in the country. And though all were here and tried to be natural and merry, only the children were free from forebodings of what the next year would bring. And it brought many changes: Don with his Reserves, Roy enlisting in the Navy, Lee in the Army. That was the year they expected Lee home from the nearby camp. His presents were under the tree and the Christmas Eve dinner ready, only to have him phone that his leave had been canceled, so that the disappointment was keener than if they had not expected him at all.

Then those dark holiday times with all three boys overseas and Jean and the babies living here at home. Ruth in uniform, coming for one Christmas, calm and clear-eyed as always, realizing perhaps more than the others that at home or abroad, waking or sleeping, Death holds us always in the hollow of his hand.

Then the clouds beginning to lift and, one by one, all coming back, Lee the last to arrive. And that grand reunion of last year after all the separations and the fears. All safe. All home. The warm touch of the hand and the welcoming embrace. Pretty Ann added to the circle. The decorating of the tree. The lights in the window. The darting in and out for last minute gift wrapping. The favorite recipes. Old songs resung. Old family jokes retold. Old laughter renewed. In joy and humility she had said, "My cup runneth over."

Recalling all this, she again grew stern with herself. How could one ask for anything more after that safe return and perfect reunion? But the contrast between then and tonight was too great. All her hopes had ended in loneliness. All her fears of approaching age had become true. One could not help the deep depression. The head may tell the heart all sorts of sensible things, but at Christmastime the heart is stronger.

She sat for a long time in front of the fire which had not warmed her. She had been on a long emotional journey and it had left her tired and spent.

From the library, loud and brazen, the phone rang. It startled her for she had never outgrown her fear of a late call. With her usual trepidation she hastened to answer. There was some delay, a far off operator's voice, and then Lee.

"That you, Mother?"

"Yes, Lee, yes. How are you?"

"Fine. Did Jeanie come?"

"No, the boys are still quarantined."

"Ruth?"

"No."

"You there alone?"

"Yes."

"Gosh, that's too bad on the old family night. Well, cheer up. I've got news for you. Our company came. She weighs seven pounds and four-teen ounces."

"What ... what did you say, Lee?"

"Our daughter arrived, Mom. Four hours ago. I waited at the hospital to see that Ann was all right."

"Why, Lee ... you never told ... we never knew ..."

"It was Ann's idea of a good joke. And listen ... we named her Margaret ... for you, Mother. Do you like it?"

"Why, yes ... *yes,* I *do* like it, Lee."

There was more, sometimes both talking at once and having to repeat. Then Lee saying, "We were wondering if you could come down in a couple of weeks. Ann thinks she'd like to have an old hand at the business around. Can you arrange it?"

"Oh, yes, Lee ... I'm sure I could."

"Good. Well, I'll hang up now. Spent enough on my call ... have to save my money to send Margaret to college. Be seeing you."

"*Lee* ..." In those last seconds she wanted desperately to put into words all the things her heart was saying. But you cannot put the thoughts garnered from a life of love and service into a sentence. So she only said: "Be a good dad, Lee. Be as good a dad as ..." She broke off, but he understood.

"I know ... I'll try. Merry Christmas, Mom."

"Merry Christmas, Lee."

She put down the receiver and walked into the living room, walked briskly as though to tell her news, her heart beating with pleasant excitement. The semicircle of chairs confronted her. With physical sight she saw their emptiness. But, born of love and imagination, they were all occupied as plainly as ever eyes had seen them. She had a warm sense of companionship. The house seemed alive with humans. How could they be so real? She swept the circle with that second sight which had been given her. Don over there ... Ruth on the hassock ... Jeanie on the davenport ... Lee and Ann in the big blue chairs ...

Suddenly she turned and walked hurriedly down the hall to the closet and came back with the little red chair. She pushed the two blue chairs apart and set the battered rocker between them. On the back hung the old brown tidy with its red cross-stitching: FOR MARGARET.

She smiled at it happily. All her numbness of spirit had vanished, her loneliness gone. This was a good Christmas. Why, this was one of the best Christmases she ever had!

She felt a sudden desire to go back to the library, to look out at the silvery garden and up to the stars. That bright one up there—it must be the one that stops over all cradles . . .

Faintly she could hear bells and voices. That would be the young crowd coming back from their caroling, so she opened the window again.

> Oh, little town of Bethlehem,
> How still we see thee lie . . .

The words came clearly across the starlit snow, singing themselves into her consciousness with a personal message:

> Yet in thy dark streets shineth
> The everlasting light
> The hopes and fears of all the years
> Are met in thee tonight.

The hopes and fears of all the years! She felt the old Christmas lift of the heart, that thankfulness and joy she had always experienced when the children were all together . . . all well . . . all home.

"My cup runneth over."

At the door of the living room she paused to turn off the lights. Without looking toward the circle of chairs, so there might come no disillusion, she said over her shoulder:

"Good-night, children. Merry Christmas. See you early in the morning."

Star Across the Tracks

MR. HARM KURTZ sat in the kitchen with his feet in the oven and discussed the world; that is to say, his own small world. His audience, shifting back and forth between the pantry and the kitchen sink, caused the orator's voice to rise and fall with its coming and going.

The audience was mamma. She was the bell upon which the clapper of his verbal output always struck. As she never stopped moving about at her housework during these nightly discourses, one might have said facetiously that she was his Roaming Forum.

Pa Kurtz was slight and wiry, all muscle and bounce. His wife had avoirdupois to spare and her leisurely walk was what is known in common parlance as a waddle. She wore her hair combed high, brushed tightly up at the back and sides, where it ended in a hard knot on top of her head. When movie stars and café society took it up, mamma said she had beat them to it by thirty-five years.

The Kurtzes lived in a little brown house on Mill Street, which meandered its unpaved way along a creek bed. The town, having been laid out by the founding fathers on this once-flowing but now long-dried creek, was called River City.

For three days of his working week pa's narrow world held sundry tasks: plowing gardens, cutting alfalfa, hauling lumber from the mill. For the other three days he was engaged permanently as a handyman by the families of Scott, Dillingham and Porter, who lived on High View Drive, far away from Mill Street, geographically, economically, socially. And what mamma hadn't learned about the Scott, Dillingham and Porter domestic establishments in the last few years wasn't worth knowing.

Early in his labors for the three families, pa had summed them up to mamma in one sweeping statement: "The Scotts ... him I like and her I don't like. The Dillinghams ... her I like and him I don't. The Porters ... both I don't like."

The Porters' house was brick colonial. The Scotts' was a rambling stone of the ranch type. The Dillinghams' had no classification, but was both brick and stone, to say nothing of stained shingles, lumber, tile, glass bricks and stucco.

The Porters had four children of school age. Also they had long curving rows of evergreens in which the grackles settled with raucous glee as though to outvie the family's noise. The grackles—and for all pa knew, maybe the young folks also—drove Mrs. Porter wild, but pa rather liked the birds. They sounded so countrylike, and he had never grown away from the farm.

Mr. Porter was a lawyer and a councilman. Mrs. Porter was a member of the Garden Club and knew practically all there was to know about flora and fauna. She went in for formal beds of flowers, rectangles and half-moons, containing tulips and daffodils in the spring and dahlias and asters later. She ruled pa with iron efficiency. With a wave of her hand she might say: "Mr. Kurtz, I think I'll have the beds farther apart this year."

And pa, telling mamma about it at night, would sneer: "Just like they was the springs-and-mattress kind you can shove around on casters."

Mrs. Scott went to the other extreme. She knew the least about vegetation of anyone who had ever come under pa's scrutiny. Assuredly he was his own boss there. Each spring she tossed him several dozen packages of seeds as though she dared him to do his worst. Once he had found rutabaga and spinach among the packages of zinnias and nasturtiums. But pa couldn't be too hard on her, for she had a little cripple son who took most of her time. And he liked the fresh-colored packages every year and the feel of the warm moist earth when he put in the seeds. The head of the house was a doctor and if he happened to drive in while pa was there, he stopped and joked a bit.

The Dillinghams' yard was pa's favorite. The back of it was not only informal, it was woodsy. Mrs. Dillingham told pa she had been raised on a farm and that the end of the yard reminded her of the grove back of her old home. She had no children and often she came out to stand around talking to pa or brought her gloves and worked with him.

"Poor thing! Lonesome," mamma said at once when he was telling her.

Mrs. Dillingham had pa set out wild crab apple and ferns and plum trees, little crooked ones, so it would "look natural." Several times she had driven him out to the country and they had brought back shooting stars and swamp candle, Dutchman's-breeches and wood violets. Pa's hand with the little wild flowers was as tender as the hand of God.

When Mr. Dillingham came home from his big department store, he was loud and officious, sometimes critical of what had been done.

In winter, the work for the High View homes was just as hard and far less interesting. Storm windows, snow on long driveways, basements to be cleaned. It was always good to get home and sit with his tired, wet feet in the oven and tell the day's experiences to mamma. There was something very comforting about mamma, her consoling "Oh, think nothing of it," or her sympathetic clucking of "Tsk...tsk...them women, with their cars and their clubs!"

Tonight there was more than usual to tell, for there had been great goings on up in High View. Tomorrow night was Christmas Eve and in preparation for the annual prizes given by the federated civic clubs, his three families had gone in for elaborate outdoor decorations.

There was unspoken rivalry among the three houses too. Pa could sense it. Mrs. Porter had asked him offhandedly, as though it were a matter of extreme unconcern, what the two other families were planning to do. And Mr.

Dillingham had asked the same thing, but bluntly. You couldn't catch pa that way, though, he reminded mamma with great glee. "Slippery as a eel!" Had just answered that the others seemed to be hitchin' up a lot of wiring.

But pa had known all along what each one was doing. And tomorrow night everybody would know. The Porters had long strings of blue lights which they were carrying out into the evergreens, as though bluebirds, instead of black ones, were settling there to stay through Christmas.

The Dillinghams had gone in for reindeer. They had ordered them made from plyboard at the mill, and tonight the eight deer, with artificial snow all over them, were prancing up the porch steps, while a searchlight on the ground threw the group into relief.

The Scotts, whose house was not so high as the others, had a fat Santa on the roof with one foot in the chimney. In a near-by dormer window there was a phonograph which would play Jingle Bells, so that the song seemingly came from the old fellow himself. It had made the little cripple boy laugh and clap his hands when they wheeled him outside to see the finished scene.

All this and much more pa was telling mamma while she ambled about, getting supper on the table.

Lillie came home. Lillie was the youngest of their three children and she worked for the Dillinghams, too, but in the department store. Lillie was a whiz with a needle, and a humble helper in the remodeling room. She made her own dresses at home and tried them on Maisie, the manikin. That was one of the store's moronic-looking models which had lost an arm and sundry other features, and Lillie had asked for it when she found they were going to discard it. Ernie, her brother, had brought it home in his car and repaired it. Now she hung her own skirts on Maisie to get their length. That was about all the good the manikin did her, for Lillie's circumference was fully three times that of the model.

The three of them sat down to eat, as Ernie would not arrive for a long time and mamma would warm things over for him. As usual, the table talk came largely from pa. He had to tell it all over to Lillie: the blue lights, the reindeer, the Santa-with-one-foot-in-the-chimney.

Lillie, who was a bit fed up with pasteboard

reindeer and synthetic Santas at the store, thought she still would like to see them. So pa said tomorrow night after Carrie got here they would all drive to High View, that he himself would like to see them once from the paved street instead of with his head caught in an evergreen branch or getting a crick in his neck under a reindeer's belly.

They discussed the coming of the older daughter and her husband, Bert, and the two little boys, who were driving here from their home in another county and planning to stay two whole nights. A big event was Christmas this year in the Mill Street Kurtz house.

After supper when Lillie started the dishes, pa went out to see to the team and mamma followed to pick out two of her fat hens for the Christmas dinner.

In the dusk of the unusually mild December evening, mamma stood looking about her as with the eye of a stranger. Then she said she wished things had been in better shape before Carrie and Bert got here, that not one thing had been done around the place to fix it up since the last time.

"That rickety old shed, pa," she said mildly. "I remember as well as I'm standin' here you tellin' Carrie you was goin' to have that good new lumber on by the next time she come."

It was as match to pine shavings. It made pa good and mad. With him working his head off, day and night! He blew up. In anyone under twelve it would have been called a tantrum. He rushed over to the tool house and got his hammer and started to yank off a rotten board.

"I'll get this done before Carrie comes," he shouted, "if it's the last thing I do."

A psychoanalyst, after much probing, might have discovered what caused pa's sudden anger. But mamma, who knew less than nothing about psychoanalysis, having only good common sense, also knew what caused it.

Pa's own regrets over his big mistake made him irritable at times. He was one of those farmers who had turned their backs on old home places during the protracted drought. Mamma had wanted to stick it out another year, but he had said no, they would move to town where everybody earned good money. So they had sold the farm and bought this little place on Mill Street, the only section of town where one could keep a cow and chickens. The very next year crops were good again and now the man who had bought the old place for so little came to

River City in a car as fine as the Dillinghams'. Yes, any casual criticism of the Mill Street place always touched him in a vital spot of his being. So he yanked and swore and jawed, more mad than ever that mamma had walked away and was not hearing him.

It was not hard to get the old boards off. Soon they lay on the ground in a scattered heap of rotting timbers. Bird and Bell, from their exposed position across the manger, snatched at the alfalfa hay, quivered their nostrils and looked disdainfully at proceedings. The cow chewed her cud in the loose-jawed way of cows and stared disinterestedly into space.

Looking at the animals of which he was so fond, pa admitted to himself he needn't have ripped the boards off until morning, but balmy weather was predicted all through Christmas. And mamma had made him pretty mad. Suddenly the fire of his anger went out, for he was remembering something Ernie had said and it tickled his fancy. The last time Carrie brought her little boys home, Ernie had told them it was bubble gum the cow was chewing and the kids had hung over the half door an hour or more waiting for the big bubble to blow out. Tomorrow night the little kids would be here and the thought of it righted the world again.

Mamma came toward him with two hens under her arms as though she wanted him to make up with her. But he fussed around among the boards, not wanting to seem pleasant too suddenly.

His flashlight lay on the ground, highlighting the open shed, and the street light, too, shone in. An old hen flew squawking out of the hay and the pigeons swooped down from the roof.

Mamma stood looking at it for quite a while, then all at once she chucked the hens under a box and hurried into the house. When she came out, she held Maisie, the manikin, in front of her and Lillie was close behind with her arms full of sheets.

"What you think you're up to?" pa asked.

"You let me be," mamma said pointedly. "I know what I'm doin'."

She set up the manikin and with deft touches Lillie draped the sheets over its body and head and arranged it so it was leaning over the manger. Then mamma put pa's flashlight down in the manger itself and a faint light shone through the cracks of the old boards.

"There!" said mamma, stepping back. "Don't

that look for all the world like the Bible story?"

"Seems like it's makin' light of it," pa said critically. "The Scotts and the Dillinghams didn't do nothin' like that. They just used Santy Clauses."

"I ain't doin' it for show, like them," mamma retorted. "I'm doin' it for Carrie's little boys. Somethin' they can see for themselves when they drive in. Somethin' they'll never forget, like's not, as long as they live."

Mamma and Lillie went out to the fence to survey their handiwork from that point. They were standing there when Ernie drove into the yard. Ernie worked for the River City Body and Fender Wreck Company, and one viewing the car and hearing its noisy approach would have questioned whether he ever patronized his own company.

They were anxious to know what Ernie thought. There were the horses nuzzling the alfalfa, the cow chewing away placidly, and the pigeons on the ridgepole. And there was the white-robed figure bending over the faint glow in the manger.

Ernie stood without words. Then he said "For gosh sakes! What in time?" The words were crude, but the tone was reverent.

"Mamma did it for the kids," Lillie said. "She wants you to fix a star up over the stable. Mrs. Dillingham gave an old one to pa."

Ernie had been a fixer ever since he was a little boy. Not for his looks had the River City Body and Fender Wreck Company hired Ernie Kurtz. So after his warmed-over supper he got his tools and a coil of wire and fixed the yellow bauble high over the stable, the wire and the slim rod almost invisible, so that it seemed a star hung there by itself.

All the next day pa worked up on High View Drive and all day mamma cleaned the house, made doughnuts and cookies with green sugar on them, and dressed the fat hens, stuffing them to the bursting point with onion dressing.

Almost before they knew it, Christmas Eve had arrived, and Carrie and Bert and the two little boys were driving into the yard with everyone hurrying out to greet them.

"Why, mamma," Carrie said. "That old shed ... it just gave me a turn when we drove in."

But mamma was a bit disappointed over the little boys. The older one comprehended what it meant and was duly awe-struck, but the younger one ran over to the manger and said:

"When's she goin' to blow out her bubble gum?"

After they had taken in the wrapped presents and the mince pies Carrie had baked, pa told them how they were all going to drive up to High View and see the expensive decorations, stressing his own part in their preparation so much that mamma said, "Don't brag. A few others had somethin' to do with it, you know." And Ernie sent them all into laughter when he called it High Brow Drive.

Then he went after his girl, Annie Hansen, and when they came back, surprisingly her brother was with them, which sent Lillie into a state of fluttering excitement.

So they all started out in two cars. Ernie and his girl and Lillie in Ernie's one seat, with the brother in the back, his long legs dangling out. Carrie and Bert took their little boys and mamma and pa. Not knowing the streets leading to the winding High View section, Bert stayed close behind Ernie's car, which chugged its way ahead of them like a noisy tugboat.

Everyone was hilariously happy. As for pa, his anger about mamma's chidings was long forgotten. All three of his children home and the two little kids. The Dillinghams didn't have any children at all for Christmas fun. *We never lost a child,* he was thinking, *and the Porters lost that little girl. Our grandkids tough as tripe, and the Scotts got that cripple boy.* It gave him a light-hearted feeling of freedom from disaster. Now this nice sight-seeing trip in Bert's good car. Home to coffee and doughnuts, with the kids hanging up their stockings. Tomorrow the presents and a chicken dinner. For fleeting moments Pa Kurtz had a warm little-boy feeling of his own toward Christmas.

Mamma, too, said she hadn't had such a good time since Tige was a pup. And when one of the little boys said he wanted to see Tige when they got back, everyone laughed immoderately.

They passed decorated houses and countless trees brightly lighted in windows. Then around the curving streets of the High View district, following Ernie's noisy lead so closely that Carrie said they were just like Mary's little lamb. Across the street from the Porters' colonial house, Ernie stopped, and they stopped too.

The evergreens with their sparkling blue lights seemed a part of an enchanted forest. Carrie said she never saw anything so pretty in her life and waxed so enthusiastic that pa reminded her again of his big part in it.

When Ernie yelled back to ask if they'd seen enough, pa waved him on. And around the curve they went to the Dillinghams'.

There were other cars in front of the houses. Pa said like as not the judges themselves were right now deciding the prizes, and by the tone of his voice one would have thought the fate of the nation hung on the decision.

At the Dillinghams', the little boys waxed more excited over the reindeer, lighted by the searchlight which threw them into snow-white relief. Yes, pa said, it was worth all the work they'd put on them.

Then to Doctor Scott's, and here the little boys practically turned inside out. For Santa himself was up on the roof as plain as day; and more, he was singing "Jingle bells...jingle bells." When he stopped, they clapped their hands and yelled up at him: "Hi, Santy! Sing more." And the adults all clapped too.

Then Ernie signaled and the little procession swung down out of High View and circled into the part of town where the blocks were prosaically rectangular and everything became smaller; yards, houses, Christmas trees.

"Look!" mamma said happily. "Ain't it nice? There ain't no patent on it. Everyone can make merry. Every little house can have its own fun and tree, just the same as the big ones."

Over the railroad tracks they went and into Mill Street, where Ernie adroitly picked his way around the mushy spots in the unpaved road, with Bert following his zigzag lead. And the trip was over.

There were Bird and Bell and the cow. There were the pigeons huddled together on the stable roof. There were the white Mary and the light in the manger, and the star. The laughter died down. Everyone got out quietly. Carrie ran her arm through her mother's. "I like yours, too, mamma," she said.

Inside, they grew merry again. Over the coffee and the doughnuts and sandwiches there was a lot of talk. They argued noisily about the prize places for the decorated houses, betting one another which ones would win. Carrie and Lillie both thought the lights in the trees were by far the most artistic. Ma and Ernie's girl were for the reindeer at Dillinghams'. But Lillie's potential beau and Ernie and Bert and the little boys were all for the Scotts' Santa Claus. Pa, as one who had been the creator of them all, stayed benignly neutral.

After a while Ernie took his girl home. Her

brother stood around on the porch awhile with Lillie and then left. The little boys hung up their stockings, with the grown folks teasing them, saying Santy could never find his way from the Scotts' down those winding streets.

Mamma and pa kept their own bedroom. Lillie took Carrie in with her. Bert went up to the attic with Ernie. Mamma made the little boys a bed on the old couch, with three chairs in front to keep them from falling out. She had no sheets left for them, but plenty of clean patchwork quilts.

In the morning there were the sketchy breakfast and the presents, including a dishpan for mamma, who had never had a new one since her wedding day; the bit and braces pa had wished for so long; a flowered comb-and-brush set for Lillie; and fully one-third of the things for which the little boys had wished.

The children could play with their new toys and the men pitch horseshoes, but mamma and the girls had to hop right into the big dinner, for everyone would be starved. Ernie's girl and her brother were invited, too, and when they came, said they could smell that good dressing clear out in the yard. The hens practically popped open in the pans and mamma's mashed potatoes and chicken gravy melted in the mouth. Oh, never did anyone have a nicer Christmas than the Kurtzes down on Mill Street.

It was when they were finishing Carrie's thick mince pies that the radio news came on, and the announcement of the prizes. So they pulled back their chairs to listen, with the girls cautioning the menfolks, "Now stick to what your bet was last night and don't anybody cheat by changing."

The announcer introduced the committee head, who gave a too wordy talk about civic pride. Then the prizes:

"The third prize of ten dollars to Doctor Amos R. Scott, 1821 High View Drive." That was Santa-in-the-chimney. And while Ernie and his group groaned their disappointment that it was only third, the others laughed at them for their poor bet.

"The second . . . twenty-five dollars . . . Mr. Ramsey E. Porter, 1484 High View Drive." The blue lights! With Carrie and Lillie wanting to know what the judges were thinking of, for Pete's sake, to give it only second, and mamma and Ernie's girl calling out jubilantly that it left only their own choice, the reindeer.

Then a strange thing happened.

"Listen, everybody."

"Sh! What's he saying?"

"The first prize ... for its simplicity ... for using materials at hand without expense ... for its sacred note and the fact that it is the personification of the real Christmas story of which we sometimes lose sight ... the first prize of fifty dollars is unanimously awarded to Mr. Harm Kurtz at 623 Mill Street."

A bomb would have torn fissures in the yard and made an unmendable shambles of the house, but it could not have been more devastating.

For a long moment they sat stunned, mouths open, but without speech coming forth, and only the little boys saying: "He said you, grandpa; he said you."

Then the hypnotic spell broke and Ernie let out a yell: "Fifty bucks, pa! Fifty bucks!"

And mamma, still dazed, kept repeating like some mournful raven, "But I just did it for the little boys."

Several got up and dashed over to the window to see again this first-prize paragon. But all they could see was Bird and Bell and the cow out in their little yard, an old dilapidated shed, and high up over it a piece of yellow glass.

In the midst of the excitement pa practically turned pale. For it had come to him suddenly there was more to this than met the eye. What would the Scotts and the Porters and the Dillinghams say? Especially Mr. Dillingham, whose expensive reindeer had won no prize at all. He was embarrassed and worried. The joy had gone out of winning the prize. The joy had gone out of the day.

The girls had scarcely finished the dishes before the Mill Street neighbors started coming to have a share in the big news. The Danish Hansens came and the Russian family from the next block, all three of the Czech families down the street, and the Negro children who lived near the mill. They were all alike to mamma. "Just folks." She made coffee and gave everyone a doughnut. In fact, they ate so many, that late in the afternoon she whipped up another batch. Also, out of honor to the great occasion, she combed her hair again in that high skinned-up way and put on a second clean apron. Two clean aprons in one day constituted the height of something or other.

"Somebody might come by," she said by way of apology.

"They'll get stuck in the mud if they do," said Ernie. "I'm the only one that knows them holes like a map."

Mamma was right. Somebody came by. All River City came by.

Soon after dusk, with the star lighted and Bird and Bell back in the shed, the cars began to drive past in unending parade. Traffic was as thick as it had ever been up on Main and Washington. You could hear talk and laughter and maybe strong words about the mud holes. Then in front of the yard, both the talk and the laughter would die down, and there would be only low-spoken words or silence. Bird and Bell pulling at the hay. The cow gazing moodily into space. The pigeons on the ridgepole in a long feathery group. White Mary bending over a faint glow in the manger. And overhead the star.

In silence the cars would drive away and more come to take their places.

Three of them did not drive away. They swung in closer to the fence and all the people got out and came into the yard. Of all things!

"Mamma, there come the Scotts and the Porters and the Dillinghams." Pa was too excited for words and hardly knew what he was doing.

But mamma was cool and went out to meet them. "Sh! They're just folks too."

The Scotts were lifting the wheeled chair out of the car, which had been custom built for it. Doctor Scott wheeled the little boy up closer so he could see the animals. Carrie's little boys ran to him and with the tactlessness of children showed him how they could turn cartwheels all around his chair.

"Why, Mr. Kurtz," Mrs. Porter was saying, "you're the sly one. Helping us all the time and then copping out the prize yourself."

Pa let it go. They would just have to believe it was all his doings, but for a fleeting moment he saw himself yanking madly at the shed boards.

Mrs. Her-I-don't-like Scott said, "It's the sweetest thing I ever saw. It made me feel like crying when I saw it."

Mrs. Dillingham said it made their decorations all look cheap and shoddy by the side of the manger scene. Even Mr. Dillingham, who had won no prize, said, "Kurtz, you certainly deserve it."

Pa knew he couldn't take any more praise. At least, not with mamma standing right there.

So he said, "I guess it was mamma's idea. She's always gettin' ideas."

Right then mamma had another one. "Will you all please to step inside and have a cup of coffee and a doughnut?"

The women demurred, but all the men said they certainly would.

So they crowded into the kitchen, mink coats and all, and stood about with coffee and doughnuts. And Lillie got up her courage and said to Mr. Dillingham, "I don't suppose you know me, but I work for you."

"Oh, yes, sure; sure I do," he said heartily, but Lillie knew he was only being polite.

"And this is a friend of mine," she added with coy bravado, "Mr. Hansen."

Mr. Dillingham said, "How do you do, Mr. Hansen. Don't tell me you work for me too."

"Yes, sir, I do," said Lillie's new beau. "Packing."

And High View and Mill Street both laughed over it.

Mrs. Scott said, "Did you ever taste anything so good as these doughnuts? You couldn't find time to make me a batch once a week, could you?" So that Mrs. Dillingham and Mrs. Porter both said quickly, "Not unless she makes me one too."

And mamma, pleased as Punch, but playing hard to catch, said maybe she could.

Mr. Porter was saying to Ernie, "You folks ought to have some gravel down here on Mill Street."

And Ernie, who wasn't afraid of anyone, not even a councilman, said with infinite sarcasm, "You're telling me?"

The big cars all drove away. Three or four others straggled by. Then no more. And pa turned off the light of the star.

The house was still again except for the adenoidal breathing of one of the little boys. Even Ernie, coming in late, stopped tromping about upstairs. Everyone had to get up early to see Bert and Carrie off and get back to work. It made pa worry over his inability to get to sleep. This had been the most exciting day in years.

Mamma was lying quietly, her heavy body sagging down her side of the bed. It took all pa's self-control to pretend sleep. Twice he heard the old kitchen clock strike another hour. He would try it.

"Mamma," he called softly.

"What?" she said instantly.

"Can't get to sleep."

"Wha's the matter?"

"Keep thinkin' of everything. All that money comin' to us. Company. Attention from so many folks. Children all home. Folks I work for all here and not a bit mad. You'd think I'd feel good. But I don't. Somethin' hangs over me. Like they'd been somebody real out there in the shed all this time; like we'd been leavin' 'em stay out when we ought to had 'em come on in. Fool notion—but keeps botherin' me."

And then mamma gave her answer. Comforting, too, just as he knew it would be. "I got the same feelin'. I guess people's been like that ever since it happened. Their conscience always hurtin' 'em a little because there wa'n't *no room for Him in the inn.*"

The Drum Goes Dead

BELLFIELD is similar to a hundred other small midwestern towns. From the air its buildings look like so many dishes clustered together on a flat table. The covered soup tureen is the community hall. The red vase in the center is the courthouse. The silver-tipped salt shaker is the water tank.

There are few changes in the ensemble from year to year. Only the tablecloth is different. There is a vivid green one for spring, a checkered green-and-tan one for summer, a mottled yellow-red-and-brown one for autumn. Just now—the day before Christmas—Nature, the busy housekeeper, had dressed the table in a snow-white cloth for the first time. It was thin, however, with bare brown places showing through, as though she must patch it soon with more white.

In one of the red-brick dish—no, *houses*—lived the Lannings. There were wreaths in the windows of the modest English-type home, a tree stood by the living-room fireplace, and a dressed turkey filled nearly half the refrigerator, just as in a thousand thousand other comfortable homes that morning.

The day was young and breakfast only now under way.

"There's just no middle ground," Grace Lanning was saying to her husband. "Either you have a Christmas complex or you don't have one. It's in the blood, I guess, transmitted from one generation to another along with other inheritances like red hair or a hooked nose or a susceptibility to hay fever. And when people have it as you and I do, Rich—and our two families had it before us, and grandparents before *that*—just *loving* the old traditions... All I can say is, I pity those who haven't inherited it."

Richard Lanning grinned understandingly at his wife's pleasant chatter as he had done for twenty years. If his usual response was purely mechanical just now, Grace Lanning failed to notice it.

They were in the breakfast nook, Richard's bulk somewhat squeezed between the table and the south side of this space-limited kitchen annex. Grace had just set the coffeepot down gingerly, and was squeezing herself between the table and the north side. "Dear me," she frowned during the maneuver, "I wish we had built this nook larger."

It was neither a new nor an original statement; some one of the four members of the family had used it as a prelude to seven-tenths of the breakfasts which had taken place within its narrow confines.

One of those other members arrived now— Alice, aged sixteen, cheerfully ready for high school's last day before vacation, but still unforgiving toward a picayunish school board that had voted to hold classes up to the last minute.

Her mother stood to let her pass to the west side of the table, saying, "I wish we'd built this nook——"

"Well!" Alice beamed. "It's really here—the day before Christmas."

The twelve-year-old member, Eldon, came noisily and hurriedly, casting himself into the remaining chair with table-quivering results, so that his mother said, *"Eldon!"* and automatically, "Dear me, I wish we'd built——"

"Gee, ain't Christmas great!" the newcomer contributed explosively.

"That's the way you feel because you've been brought up like that," his mother was definiteness itself. "Dad and I were just saying so." As a matter of truthfulness the mechanism of Dad's mouth, throat and tongue had been engaged entirely with buckwheat cakes and not conversation. But long-married women are like that. "My family all went to Grandma Rowe's as long as she lived. Dad's folks always had the rest of their relatives..." She talked on cheerily, reminiscences bubbling from her like the coffee in the percolator.

Grace Lanning was healthy, normal, energetic. She enjoyed festivities, liked tackling a day that held involved duties, untangling its loose ends and tying them in a finished bow-knot at its close. One would know that her packages were all tied, cards mailed, meals planned.

From where he sat, Richard Lanning could see the poplars bending in the stiff December wind, and the brown-brick rear of the Shellhorn home. He gazed at them thoughtfully, his mind engrossed.

"Dad, *you* don't look very Christmasy!"

Alice had noticed, then. No, how could he be Christmasy this year? How could anyone, for that matter? But he did not say all this. No one but a cad could destroy the family's enthusiasm. So he turned her observation off with banter.

Breakfast finished, there was the usual commotion when the children and their father left, even an extra amount due to countless directions about packages and errands. Then Richard Lanning was walking alone down the street to the Bellfield State Bank where he had been cashier for so many years.

Stories are seldom written about the Richard Lannings. Stage plays do not revolve around them. The screen consistently ignores them. To work steadily and honestly at one business, to love one woman and no other, to be neither the target for criticism because of wealth nor the object of sympathy because of poverty does not make for colorful drama. But there are so many small-town Richard Lannings.

No, there was nothing dramatic about the cashier of the Bellfield bank walking to business every morning of his life, returning every evening to Grace and the two children, excepting as he saw in those intervening hours all the joys and sorrows, pleasures and worries of the community pass in front of that grilled window, and in doing so, became a part of them.

It was of these people he was thinking as he walked the five blocks this gray morning, scorning the car for so short a distance. "That's why old Professor Shellhorn is still so spry," he was wont to say. "He's never stopped walking and so never lost the use of his legs."

It was cold and windy, and even though the air felt damp, there had been very little snow. Nature had been parsimonious with her good moisture these last few years. By that withholding she had ruined three corn crops, lessened pasturage, killed many of the town's fine old trees, and created havoc in the community.

Richard Lanning thought of it soberly as he picked his way along the snowy walk. On every block were houses and garages that needed painting, the trunks of dead trees that should be cut. The general rundown appearance of the little town lay heavily on his mind.

The depression—the one with the capital *D* —had never quite left the community. Just as they had been pulling out of it, the drouth had settled down over the land like a smothering blanket. "But *our* county *always* has good corn," everyone had said at first. "Sometimes farther out West there's drouth, but never *here.*" And yet this was the third bad year for the corn which had come up each season with so much promise. Even the wheat harvested earlier this year had been varied—good in sections, but streaked with rust on some of the best farms.

This past early summer, soaking rains had come and the corn had stood green and tall in the fields. Then, in a single day, a hot wind had blown out of the south, like the blast from some satanic smithy's forge, and undone all the work of the springtime. The intense heat fairly boiled the water at the corn's roots, steaming it up into the tender stalks and virtually cooking them, even brewing a poison in them so that the farmers who turned their cattle into the brown fields had lost some and saved others only by a desperate fight.

It was as though Providence would not help these men in the lifting of their burdens. They had worked so hard, so faithfully, their hope always renewed at the spring planting. And Nature would not do her share. Only a few years before there had been ample rains, fine corn, fat cattle on the rolling hills, the big barns and silos filled with feed. Now for three years there were half crops, poor pastures, thin animals, peeling paint on the barns.

As in all agricultural sections, the farmers' plight was the townspeople's worry also, so closely were their businesses intertwined. And this was the day to say Merry Christmas across the bank's counter to these people who were not merry, whose every waking hour was filled with financial worry.

Not only was this community troubled, but the whole world was in turmoil. Nations were at other nations' throats. But no one must forget to sing a mawkish "Peace on earth!" There were countless dissensions in our own country: quarrels over parties and creeds and divergent lines of thought. But every participant must stop his squabbling long enough to mouth a hypocritical "Good will to men!"

That night at the community hall the children would sing, "All is calm, all is bright." There would be a silver star at the top of a tree, symbol of good cheer and tranquillity. And there was neither cheer nor tranquillity here or anywhere else.

Well, he himself would not be a part of it. For nearly a dozen years he had been Santa Claus at the program, just why, he had never stopped to question—merely one of those ruts into which a small-town man slips. But no more! Charlie Pearson had promised to go through the farce tonight. For the whole thing was a travesty under these conditions. It would be more honest to abandon the celebration of the day temporarily. Face the facts. Decide that until things were somewhat righted, there would be no tree, no star, no gifts, no carols. When misery and worry had abated, when the human mind was ready to receive the thought of these symbols again—the heart respond to the harmony for which they stood—then renew the traditional services. It was dishonorable to pretend, hypocritical to mouth these prayers and sing of peace.

With honest self-analysis Richard Lanning knew this was a frightening change in his way of thinking. He could scarcely believe that he was the same person who, as a boy, had so loved the season. Grace had referred to his family at breakfast time. He had a sudden vision now of the farmhouse, the snow banked high against its old stone walls, but within them a hospitality as warm as the fires from the great wood stoves. The wreaths had been made from the pines in the yard, and the gifts had been simple. There had been a tree and a star and Christmas carols around the old piano. There had been a better feeling then. And people had seemed kinder. They had taken their disappointments with better spirit, pulled themselves through their difficulties with more independence and courage.

As a boy in that environment he had fairly worshiped the Christmas time. As a young married man he had not lost his pleasure in it. When his children came he had thrilled to a renewal of it through them. Even now, he had no intention of pricking the bubble of their enthusiasm. Let them enjoy themselves while they could. Only a few short seasons ago he, too, had felt with them the spirit of the day.

He would put on a good front now, but he wanted more than that. He wished deeply that he could feel a measure of their fervor as once he had done. But the capacity to do so seemed gone. Something of the spirit was dead within him, and the death of the spirit is a grievous thing.

He was at the bank now. Two of the little staff of five arrived as he did. George Adams, the wise-cracking son of the president, facetiously greeting the no-longer-young Elsie Rouse with:

" 'Twas the night before Christmas and all through
    the house
Not a creature was stirring, not even Miss Rouse."

Elsie put a wreath of holly in each service window, with George making flippant remarks about changing it to mistletoe if the new teacher came in. Richard Lanning opened the vault. The others arrived. The voice of the president issued from an inner office. The nine-o'clock mail was opened. Everyone was busy. Town people began straggling in, a farmer or two, a small trickle that would change later in the day to a stream. There was a deposit made, some interest paid, cream checks cashed. Your country bank cashier has no specific duties, no department over which he presides exclusively as does his city contemporary. He receives money and pays it out, makes loans and adroitly refuses them, takes his turn at the books, clerks at many a farm sale, advises his customers when to buy hogs, to marry, and to have their tonsils out.

So now if Richard Lanning put aside the pessimistic thoughts which had enwrapped his mind like a dark cloak, it was only because some of these various tasks blotted them out. Even so, he was vaguely conscious of the castoff garment which he must wear again, sensed that back of the meticulous handling of his work there was a longing for more shining armor.

Although there were fussy customers who

would have tried the soul of Job, to all who
stood in front of his window he was courteous
without regard to age, financial standing or previous condition of servitude. It was one of his
assets. So he spoke pleasantly of the holiday to
everyone.

"How does it seem to be home for Christmas?"

"Going to your daughter's as usual?"

It was midforenoon when Miss Jarman came
in. She had been a teacher, but home for many
years now, caring for her father, the county's
last Grand Army man. Richard Lanning could
remember how Marshal Jarman always rode a
horse at the head of the Memorial Day procession, holding in the prancing steed with taut
rein as he surreptitiously spurred it into more
cavorting.

"Merry Christmas, Miss Jarman." (Yes, say
it, even though the pension is all they have.)
"How's your father?"

"Father's out in the car."

"I'll step out to see him. George, you take
care of Miss Jarman's wants."

This was part of the ritual when the old man
favored the bank with his presence at the curb.
He had been a leading property-holder in a long-

gone day, but the only deed in his tin box now was the one to the little G.A.R. hall which he grimly refused to turn over to the upstart veterans of two later wars.

He found the old man in overcoat, cap, muffler and mittens, a blanket around his knees. His mind was clear, his body a sapless leaf quivering before the coming wind in the trees. He was pleased at the attention given him, shook Richard's hand through the car window. "Merry Christmas," his old voice croaked.

"Merry Christmas," Richard responded. "But not so very merry, with bad crops, everybody feeling hard up, and the world in a mess."

"You know," the old man quavered, "I been thinkin' about all the Christmases I've seen. If I live tonight, this will be my ninety-fourth." He chortled, as though the joke would be on someone if he made it through the night. "Been tryin' to remember as many's I could."

His voice held no vibrancy but his mind clung tenaciously to its line of thought. "Sometimes I know the years and sometimes not, but you'd be surprised how many I can recollect—dozens of 'em."

You had to humor him. "Which was your best one?"

Immediately Richard Lanning was wondering why he had asked him. It would only start him off on a flood of I-recollects— Yes, there it came.

"Well, now ... When I was seven—that must 'a' been 1854—Mother was tryin' to hold our bodies and souls together, promisin' us a good Christmas and yet not knowin' where it was comin' from. And what do you think happened? My pappy come home from the Far West. One of the 'forty-niners, he was.

"Trampin' in after dark that way, us young-uns got him all mixed up with old Sandy Claus. Yes, sir!" The bleary old eyes peered at Richard. "Can recollect most every Christmas, *includin'* the one when we had the big bonfire at Atlanty, Georgy, before startin' out with Sherman on that little hoofin' jaunt we took to the sea. But the one I recollect as the best of all was the one when I took my bride to our first home. It was a soddy ... only one room but snug as could be and we thought it was about the nicest home a-body could have. Our first Christmas there. . . ."

He would have gone on endlessly if his daughter had not arrived.

Back at work with something of the old man's rambling talk still in his mind, Richard Lanning found himself asking his next customer: "What was the best Christmas *you* ever had?"

It was Hulda Bornheimer, who had worked for them when Alice was born. She was a farmer's wife now, and today was cashing her cream check.

Her fat red face lighted. "Oh, there's lots of good ones, Mr. Lanning. Maybe the best was when I was a slip of a girl and hirin' out already yet to a family up beyond Mapleton. They wasn't much on Christmas; kind of laughed at doin' anything extra. And my folks was so much for it. Always a little tree—*Tannen-baum* we called it—and candles on it and peppernuts. And singin' *'Stille Nacht, Heilige Nacht'* and drinkin' a toast in kümmel.

"I was goin' home, but there come a big snow and I had to give up the thoughts. Then Pa come for me through it, shovelin' the drifts, and when we got there finally and I opened the kitchen door and smelled the fresh coffee-cake and Christmas cookies and saw the little green tree on the table and knew I was *home*—I guess *that* one couldn't be beat."

A trucker brought in a shipment of supplies and stopped for his pay.

"Well, Jake, how goes it?"

"Not so good. The missis has to have an operation."

"That's tough. Christmas doesn't seem like it used to."

"No. It don't that."

"Just for fun, Jake, tell me what Christmas you remember best."

Jake took off his cap and ran his hand through the ring of graying hair which circled his head like a fuzzy halo. "Don't laugh, but you asked for it. When I was a scrubby kid my mother used to get us all around her and read us the Bible story on Christmas Eve. Once when I'd gone to bed and was asleep, some young folks who took a notion to go around singin' woke me up with that there 'Hark! the Herald Angels.' From where I lay I could see a big star lookin' in at me, and kidlike, I thought the music was comin' from the sky like in the story, and I was plumb scared." He shifted tired feet and leaned heavily on the shelf of the grilled window.

"But that ain't all...'. In 'ninety-eight, we'd just got to Camp Columbia near Marianao, Cuba, the day before Christmas. Had breakfast aboard ship while it was still dark, and one of our company had fell through a hatchway and was killed. Made us blue as indigo. Day was sticky hot. Christmas rations was goin' to be poor—canned salmon, potatoes and coffee—all that junk we had then. None o' this stylish board the army has now for us Spanish-American volunteers. Everybody was homesick.

"Went to bed and in the middle of the night was woke from a sound sleep by that same 'Hark! the Herald Angels.' Some of the band boys was playin' and some singin' it. Wakin' up that way out of a sound sleep, hearin' that Christmas song, I'll be darned if there wasn't the biggest star you ever saw hangin' low in the sky and shinin' through the tent. It took me a long time to come to and find out I wasn't that same scared little kid at home hearin' music out of the sky. I ain't ashamed to say I shed a tear or two into that old army blanket, I was that homesick."

He began asking others.

"What's the Christmas you remember best, J.B.?"

The man was a merchant, hard-working, taciturn. He put the deposit receipt in his billfold, squinted into it as though the answer were there in its dingy interior. "I guess the time I was in Alaska, Dick, when I was a young fellow. Was up at the little town of Candle then, up above the Circle. All the residenters decided to give a Christmas dinner to the boys up the creek and any the rest of the world that might happen along. Table was decorated with green, and candles lighted; had baked fish and ptarmigan stew. Eighty white folks et and twenty-five Eskimos.

"A pretty decent orderly crowd, I'll say, those miners dressed in parkas and mukluks. Not half the rowdy goin's-on you'd expect. Guess the singin' Christmas songs round the table sort of got them thinkin' of home."

All day they came and went, these common, ordinary small-town folk. And all day, if the circumstances allowed, Richard Lanning asked his question.

To a young girl who had taken a maid's place in a nearby city instead of a university course when her hope of schooling vanished with the drying corn: "Which was the best Christmas you ever had, Marian?"

"Oh, Mr. Lanning, *this* one—to get home for the first time."

To a little old lady with an income of eight dollars a month: "What was your best Christmas, grandma?"

"Oh, my! Just any of them, I guess, when the children were at home."

By the middle of the afternoon there was no time for social conversation. The cashier was a machine, working almost as mechanically as the one clicking near him under the hand of Elsie Rouse.

"All we need now to add to old-home week are the examiners or old scholastic Shellhorn," young Adams took time to say.

So soon afterward that they were obliged to avoid each other's eyes for fear of laughing, old Professor Shellhorn came in, his cane thump-thumping across the little lobby, with George muttering under his breath, "And what is the subject of our lecture today, professor?"

"Merry Christmas!" The old man nodded gravely to them all. "Christmas time again, good friends." He spread out his arms in theatrical gesture, quoted grandiloquently: " 'Now good cheer and welcome. Not a cup of drink must pass without a carol; the beasts, fowl and fish come to a general execution, and the corn is ground to dust for the bake house and the pastry.' You see, I have been reading again as I have for many years the Christmas customs of old England. Those were merry days, according to authentic information." The pedantic old man! "It was several centuries ago that this was written anent the Christmas season:

" 'The maskers and the mummers make the merry
     sport
   But if they lose their money, their drum goes
     dead.'

"I have been telling my daughter-in-law that while the original thought was not quite the same as my modern application, it had held good for these hundreds of years. We are all more or less like that, are we not? We're maskers and mummers having a merry time but if we lose our money or our crops or a friend, the drum goes dead. It takes a great deal of spirit and courage to beat away as though nothing had happened, does it not?"

He cashed his small check and left, thumping his cane along the lobby floor.

It was closing time. The shutters were drawn, the big doors locked. But there were two hours yet of work behind the scenes.

A few feathery snowflakes fluttered into the gathering winter dusk as Richard Lanning walked home, tired from the busy day, his own worries and the burdens of the people still with him. It was true—the drum goes dead.

The lights of the small-town stores shone across the walk. Others twinkled up and down the familiar old streets. He had glimpses of Christmas trees in all the houses—the brick ones and the frame, the well-kept ones and the shabby ones with peeling paint. All the homes of the community seemed striving for traditional cheer and good will. It brought to mind the experiences the customers had told him. And suddenly the thought struck him that through everything they had said ran the theme of *home:* "When the children were all home." "Thought I was a kid again at home." "Took my bride to my home." Christmas, by magical invisible cords, bound everyone to his home. They were almost interchangeable, those words—*Christmas* and *home*.

And here he was at his own, brightly lighted, with wreaths in the windows and the little tree sparkling. Alice met him at the door.

"Dad, you've got to be Santa Claus yourself again. Charlie Pearson just phoned. He broke a bone in his wrist this afternoon. He's got it in splints or a sling or something. He said every little kid would know who he was with his arm that way, and besides who ever saw a Santa Claus with a busted arm."

Thinking how incongruous was the combination of his low spirits and the mask of the merry patron saint gave him his first hearty laugh of the day. Oh, well, what was it old Shellhorn had said about the maskers and the mummers?

Dinner was pushed along a bit hastily on account of the program. Eldon was feverishly excited, frankly anticipating a rifle in the morning, reminding all and sundry that if he *was* getting one, not to forget the shot. Alice was equally anticipatory, but putting up what she fondly thought was a more sophisticated front. Grace called the roll of the baskets she had taken here and there, the little packages she had delivered, the various tasks performed. All the loose ends of the day were tied and she was vocally percolating about them.

Community Hall, the covered soup tureen of a building, was gaily lighted, decorated, and surcharged with the electricity of youthful spirits.

Santa Claus, secreted in the wings until such time as he would walk out to the tree, could smell the resinous odor of the pines, could see through an aperture the upturned faces of the children of the community at the front of the room, their elders behind them. All the people who had known losses and hard times were out there: old Professor Shellhorn, who had lost his money; Hulda, whose best team had died; Jake, whose missis had to have the operation; old Grandma Smith, whose children had gone away. From the wings he could see them all, their care-worn faces relaxed, their eyes on the performing children.

It was the typical yearly program, small-town-ish and laughable, unless one knows and understands the little cross-roads of the country: Mrs. Henry Neiman rendering her annual solo, bursting forth from the wings like a palpitating *Brunhilde;* fat Amy Anderson reciting an adenoidal piece which sounded like "forever adda-day, till the washall crubble to ruin and boulder in dustaway"; red-headed Joey Myers doing a staccato machine-gun version of "On-Comet-on-Cupid-on-Donder-and-Blitzen"; a group of tiny Christmas elves arriving on the stage to sing "Here we come tripping," and true enough, in gazing up to the awesome distances of the rafters above them, losing their balance and going down like dominoes; then the tableau of the manger scene, with a youthful Joseph swathed in Turkish towels standing first on one foot and then the other, grinning sheepishly at the audience; with a husky two-year-old Babe peeping up over the side of the manger and being pushed back determinedly by the supposedly gentle Mary.

Then a song dying away gave the cue for Santa Claus to proceed with the important work of the evening: the calling of names for the packages under the tree.

There was no great mystery over the impersonation. Almost anyone in the audience except the tiniest children, awe-struck and believing, could have told that Richard Lanning was the patron saint. So that when he picked up a flat package to read his own name, saying with great gusto, "I'll see that Mr. Lanning gets this later," and slipped it into one of the red pockets, a boy called back: "Open it yourself, now."

"Yah! Open it yourself, Santy Lanning," another said, with the whole audience laughing.

It was a queer Christmas gift—a mere booklet of drawing-paper with a school-made design on its cover. Inside, it said that the grades and high-school by unanimous vote had chosen Mr. Richard Lanning as Bellfield's most helpful citizen, counselor and friend. This was to tell him so, and to wish him a very merry Christmas and many more. Signed by classes, with all the children's names.

Santa Claus, grateful for his merry mask which covered no little surprise and a bit of emotion, thanked the boys and girls on behalf of Richard Lanning, who, he was sure, would always try to merit their respect.

And now the whole school was singing the last song.

> "O little town of Bethlehem!
>   How still we see thee lie;
>   Above thy deep and dreamless sleep
>   The silent stars go by."

The high sweet voices rose, tremulous with childish fervor:

> "Yet in thy dark streets shineth
>   The everlasting Light;
>   The hopes and fears of all the years
>   Are met in thee tonight."

The man who had been feeling that Christmas gifts should be abandoned until the world could give and receive them with better heart was looking into the glowing faces of the children who had just made him a gift of cheap

drawing-paper—a priceless gift of heart-warming friendship and trust.

And so suddenly that it seemed a new thought —though it was as old as the silent stars—a bright-colored strand wove itself across the gray warp of his mind. *The world was not in chaos to these children.* Through their eyes it was still the same world of limited dimensions he and these other burdened people had known as children, and because this was so, it was still a good world.

Humanity must hang fast to its faith and its hope. It must never let them go as long as there remained in the world a child and a song, a gift and a star.

Peculiarly, he had a sensation of lightening spirits. Nothing had changed materially. The same losses, disappointments and burdens awaited the community outside like dark-omened birds of prey, but they seemed less forbidding now. He felt mentally strengthened, emotionally comforted. He could carry on as "helpful citizen, counselor and friend."

Everyone went home—to the big houses and the little ones, the well-kept ones and those with peeling paint—the homes which, God be thanked, were still a part of the bulwark of the nation.

The snow was covering the unfruitful corn lands and the green winter wheat with its life-giving moisture, reminding all that another spring would come. The Christmas stars hung low in the winter sky. Up the street the high clear voices of carolers were singing "No-el, No-el."

Santa Claus, whose musical voice was not the type one would call of concert quality, suddenly broke forth into a lusty off-key version of "Drums in My Heart," so that Grace said, "For goodness' sake, Rich, being Santa and getting the school children's praise must have upset you! Not touched in the head, are you?"

"No," he grinned, "just beginning to feel young and hopeful and a bit Christmasy."

Youth Is All of an Up-and-Coming

MANY years ago, this story was told to me by an elderly woman and her daughter. Although the setting and some of the details have been fictionized, the main theme of the story—a bit of early Nebraska drama—remains as they told it. At that time, both mother and daughter related it, one breaking in on the other in her earnestness, but for clarity's sake, it is here given as the daughter might have written it:

The Christmas mystery over at the Stoltenberg house has been solved. The odd thing about it is that the Stoltenberg sons and daughters and grandchildren are entirely ignorant of the solution—and always will be. Only Mother and I, their next door neighbors, know what happened. And we shall never tell.

One never knows when he will run head-on into a bit of drama—and it was real drama which unfolded before our eyes Christmas morning. You eat and sleep, work and play. The sun comes up and the sun goes down. Life seems monotonous, people ordinary. And then suddenly the curtain of life is drawn, and for a brief moment someone stands before you with all the characteristics of a player doing his part. If that someone has the familiar features of a person whom you have long looked upon as one with no dramatic moments in his experience, astonishment is proportionately keen.

So when the curtain came up on Christmas day, revealing old Mr. and Mrs. Henry Stoltenberg as the leads in a two-act play, with a half century between Acts I and II, it had the effect of an electric shock.

To pick up the threads of the story, one must go back to the summer when the two moved next door to us.

They were a good old couple, Mr. and Mrs. Stoltenberg, so solid and substantial that they illustrated the dog-eared phrase, "salt of the earth," about as aptly as any pair could do. We knew them by sight for many years, seeing "Pa" Stoltenberg driving his car into town, sitting stiffly at the wheel and staring straight ahead, making hard work of his late exchange of two stolid mares for an intricate piece of machinery, and with "Ma" Stoltenberg sitting heavily in

the back seat, her huge bulk the obvious reason
for the tandem mode of travel. And driving so
into town, they were representative of ten thousand couples in the trans-Missouri States—one
pair from the countless numbers that had
crossed the Missouri and forded the Platte or
the Blue or the Elkhorn in prairie schooners and
located on lonely prairie claims, but living to
drive automobiles over paved roads into thriv-
ing towns. In those early days their assets, like
the others, had been little more than a team and
wagon and plow. And *youth!* But when Mother
and I first knew who they were, they had acquired two hundred acres of rich, cultivated
land, and many fine cattle and hogs. And *age!*

The Stoltenbergs had raised five sons and
daughters. Like the parents, the five were thrifty
and respectable. There were two farmers among
them, and a printer, and a "Rosa" and a
"Minnie" who taught school. Yes, Henry and
Elsa Stoltenberg had done well in the years since
they had first stepped from the prairie schooner
and turned the virgin sod where the long grass
rippled in the wind.

And so, after seeing the old couple drive past
our home for many years, we learned that they
had come to town on a summer afternoon and

purchased the big brick house on the corner next to us—an old-fashioned, outmoded house with colored windowpanes and jigsaw pillars and a wealth of flutings and furbelows. They did a little remodeling for the next few weeks and then settled down comfortably as our next-door neighbors. From that time on we knew them no longer by sight and reputation only, for your small town is a friendly, garrulous place and neighbors are their brothers' keepers. Whether or not we liked them, we had to accept them, for they immediately adopted Mother and me as close friends. But we did like them. We liked them immensely. From that time Mrs. Stolten-berg, with no previous call from us, appeared smilingly at our side door with *kaffee-kuchen* from which there rose all the hot savory odors of the spices of Araby, we liked her golden good-ness. And from the time Mr. Stoltenberg, with gnarled tender fingers and soothing German phrases, worked over our little injured dog, he was our friend.

Occasionally the two would come over to our porch in the lush summer evenings, "Pa" walk-ing agilely enough for his nearly seventy years, "Ma" heavily because of her bulk. They told us everything about themselves. With childlike garrulity they turned their lives inside out for us to hear. They told us of the trip from eastern Illinois and of the red-eyed oxen that had brought them. They described in definite detail the long, wearisome journey through the tangles of wild plum and sumac, the endless days of lurching across miles of waving grass and sunflowers. They pictured their first sod house, for us and the misery of the grasshopper raid. With simple and unabashed frankness they told of the horror of childbirth without a doctor and of the grief that gripped them when their first baby died. Together they had buffeted storm and blizzard. Together they had known grief and happiness.

They were extremely fond of each other. And they were childlike in the enjoyment of the fussy new house.

The Stoltenberg children were loyalty personified. On numerous Sundays they arrived with baskets and vociferous offspring, and every birthday was a noisy feasting day next door to us.

But if previous holidays had been joyful occasions, Christmas was the sum total of all the others. For weeks before that first Christmas, wreaths made their appearance in the fussy windows tipped by colored glass. The largest tree procurable touched the ornate ceiling of the parlor, big logs were fitted to the two fireplaces. Greens and tissue paper intertwined the handrail of the stairway. Pa Stoltenberg deftly picked two geese and a turkey. Apparently Ma baked everything to be found in her six thick cookbooks. Every opening of her kitchen door was a cinnamon-scented breath of the coming of Christmas.

We saw Rosa and Minnie arrive, bundle-laden, to be enveloped in the long thin arms of Pa and the short fat ones of Ma out on the front steps. The old folks' faces were shining. "Christmas," Ma called over to us later from the back porch, "it is the time for all mankind to be at peace. Is it not so?"

We saw the middle-aged "boys" arrive with their families—all to be greeted by the same noisy, all-embracing welcome. If the telling of these sights places Mother and me in the light of peeping neighbors, we can be forgiven. For not always, these days, may one look upon such old-fashioned family celebrations. And Mother and I, who had once been participants in such scenes ourselves, were lonely.

It was some time after the Christmas festivities before the old couple, in an evening of reminiscences, mentioned the name of the little town in Illinois from which they had come. It was Macyville. And when I told them we had a friend teaching there in their old town of long ago, they were deeply interested. They inquired at length about her, but when they found she had lived there but a scant twenty years, they lost interest. It had been nearly a half century since it was their home. But it made an added bond between us. "She seldom writes us," I told them. "Instead she sends us a paper every little while with some item in it about herself, and when the next one arrives, I'll bring it over for you to read." So when one came not long afterward, I carried it over as soon as Mother and I had read the little blue-penciled item pertaining to our friend. We saw the old folks through the window afterward, their heads close together scanning the little sheet.

Each following autumn Mother and I grew to look forward to the coming Christmas festivities next door to us. It was as though we were onlookers at some occasion so happy that the joy overflowed a little into our own yard. And not only did the joy come our way, but what was more practical, a portion of all that wonderful baking. Mrs. Stoltenberg could not have gone through the Christmas season without sharing with us. "Christmas—it is the time for all mankind to be at peace. Is it not so?"

In the fourth autumn of their town residence, with Mr. Stoltenberg seventy-two and his wife sixty-eight, something came over them which Mother and I could not understand. Something seemed dampening their spirits, weighing on their minds. The depression did not seem to arise from physical sources, for Pa worked as vigorously as ever getting ready for winter, and Ma turned out her savory baking and journeyed heavily as always over her fussy house.

We found ourselves discussing the change in the old folks often. Small town people are like that. A little too curious, perhaps, but sympathetic. We wondered if one of the children had been giving the old folks some worried hours. However, there was not the least hint of any trouble.

But the old folks sat on the side porch and talked long and gravely in the warm Indian summer evenings of October. Sometimes we inadvertently heard argumentative tones. All through November we sensed that something obsessed their minds. Perhaps it was the plans for the eventual division of the estate, we said.

To be sure, it was none of our business, but after all, it was a little painful to think of the devoted old couple having either worry or trouble in the sunset of their long peaceful life together.

The Christmas season was approaching, with no apparent resumption of the vast preparations for it which we had grown to enjoy, if vicariously. At any mention of the coming holiday, Ma would sigh heavily without much comment. Small as it might have seemed to an outsider, to us who knew their devotion to the greatest holiday of them all, the absence of preparation was monumental in scope.

And then one evening in the dim twilight of a December day they came over, and as though it were our right and privilege to know, told us that they had just experienced a great relief, for after many weeks of discussion they had definitely decided to drive in the car back to Macyville before Christmas.

We were genuinely pleased at the news—and immeasurably relieved. After all, they had merely worried over one of those states of indecision which make some people genuinely ill.

"And your friend—will she be there?" they were both asking.

No, we were sorry to tell them—our friend went away each Christmas, and she would probably be gone by this time. But it was apparently no disappointment to them, for neither commented.

"And you'll be visiting relatives, won't you?" We were rejoicing with them to think they would see their kindred after nearly a half century.

No, there were no relatives left, they said. Pa had been an only son of Heinrich Stoltenberg, a well-to-do merchant, and his wife, Johanna, but they had been gone these countless years.

"And I am once Elsa Haas—an orphan," Ma said. And in an apologetic aside, she added: "Many years I work for his mother—since I am twelve." Ah! Those spicy cinnamon rolls and nutty *pralines*. No wonder the young Henry had succumbed!

It would be a fine trip for them both, we assured them enthusiastically. But strangely enough, there seemed no answering enthusiasm. They only sat with unaccustomed silence as we chattered about the trip.

"Oh—I know not," Pa said dubiously, when we had both exclaimed at length over the anticipated event. "It's a long, long journey. Better

I should stay in my own yard in cold weather—
with the Christmas not far away."

"But you'll meet old friends," we persisted,
"and be so happy to renew their acquaintance."

But Pa was not to be convinced. "No, no."
He shook his small gray head. "Not old friends
—not old friends any more yet after all the
years."

"Anyway, you can visit all the old scenes of
your youth, and that will pay you for the long
trip," was Mother's cheerful contribution. But
why should all the optimism concerning the trip
come from Mother and me?

"Yes, yes—I will be returning to the old
scenes," he admitted.

"As a murderer returns to the scenes of his
crime," I laughed.

And oddly enough, the moment I had uttered
it, the joke seemed in terribly poor taste. For
both he and Ma failed to relinquish their deep
seriousness, and the old man was saying, "Ah,
well, we make mistakes," and Ma was adding
the echo to his thought, "Yah—youth is all of
an up-and-coming when the blood is warm."
And they rose and walked heavily back to the
fussy old house.

Gradually, by what means we did not know,

it grew upon us that the trip was to be a thing of duty, that by making it there was to be restitution of some sort. A chance remark, a bit of suggestive thought, and we finally felt we saw the solution take shape. "It's the dead parents," we decided. They had not wanted the marriage between the two. Perhaps they had thought the only son of a well-to-do merchant would be stepping out of his rank to marry the little Elsa Haas, orphan. There had been some kind of a break and the two had never gone back. "And they've grown sensitive about it in their old age," I told Mother. "I'll wager the whole long trip is being made for no bigger reason than to put flowers on the graves of his parents, or something equally as child-like." It seemed a simple solution. And yet—why should they go at the Christmas time?

On a crisp morning they started—not happily. Pa looked longingly up at the fussy gingerbread house after locking the big door, and Ma sighed when she climbed heavily into the back seat of the car. Then they were off.

In time a postcard came to us with a pale reproduction of Macyville's main street on one side and a painfully scrawled message from Pa Stoltenberg on the other. Ma Stoltenberg, too, had sent us a card—a cheap Christmas card with a green wreath on a frosted background. There was no message, but it needed none. In fancy we could hear: "Christmas—it is the time for all mankind to be at peace. Is it not so?"

Christmas was to be on Friday. On Tuesday night, with cold-looking clouds scudding across a darkening sky, they drove into the yard.

Mother and I hurried over with words of welcome and bowls of hot soup. We found them tired, but apparently very happy. Ma Stoltenberg said enthusiastically she must do a whole week's work now in two days. Pa said he must get the tree and pick his geese. They were just as they had been before those months of apparent depression.

The old Christmas festivities were celebrated next door as they had never been. Never had there been so many wreaths, such a huge tree. Every opening of the back door was a cinnamon-flavored, clove-scented breeze of delight. On Christmas morning the children drove in and were enveloped in the long thin and the short fat arms of their parents. There was a great deal of noise and laughter.

Strangely enough, with our Christmas mail came one of the occasional newspaper messages from our teacher friend. It contained the account of her illness and an editor's gracious comment that all the townspeople were sorry that the annual holiday vacation of so faithful a teacher must be spent on the sick bed.

We read the article through, and then, because the Stoltenbergs had just been there in Macyville, it gave us the unusual interest of looking over the rest of the little sheet. There would most certainly be a write-up of the old couple's return, I told Mother—a pleasant laudation of the way they had gone West as bride and groom in a covered wagon, and returned after prosperous years in an automobile. But we could find nothing. Up and down the columns I looked, faintly provoked that an editor should pass by so dramatic an item.

Through the window we could see the green wreaths and catch a glimpse of the great tree next door. Even with the house closed, we could hear the sounds of revelry from the Stoltenbergs. Never had they enjoyed such a Christmas party.

And then—quite suddenly—I saw the name "Stoltenberg" halfway down a column on the last page. It jumped out at me with all the clarity which a familiar name possesses in a maze of unfamiliar ones. I stared at the item. It was a moment before I could sense the import of it. The words danced grotesquely in front of my eyes. It was incredible. But there it was in clear-cut type. I walked over to Mother, and with a finger that was not quite steady, pointed silently to the brief item. It said: "Henry Stoltenberg . . . aged 72. Elsa Haas . . . aged 68." And the names were under the caption, MARRIAGE LICENSES.

Christmas—it is a time of peace for all mankind. Is it not so?

The Man Who Caught the Weather

H E lived next door to us when I was a girl— old Mr. Parline. To be sure, his wife lived there, too, but we never saw very much of her. She was one of the immaculate housewives of that day, whose life was bounded by the hundred small tasks of a home into which the modern button-pushing conveniences had not come. A shy, effacing woman she was—"mousy" describes her too well to abandon the term for its mere triteness. Mr. Parline was the one who did the talking, who neighbored with the rest of us, who came to the back door bringing us gifts from his garden.

The Parline house sat in the midst of trees and flowers like Ceres among her fruits. We were just then emerging from the dark age of fences into the enlightened era of open lawns. By your fenced or fenceless condition you were known as old-fashioned or up-to-date. One by one the picket and the fancy iron and the rough board fences on our street had gone down before the god of Fashion. Mr. Parline, alone, retained his—a neat picket, painted as white as the snowballs that hung over it, Juliet-like, from their green foliage balconies.

The shrubbery was not so artistically placed as that of to-day. We had not learned to group it against houses and walls, leaving wide stretches of lawn. Single bushes dotted Mr. Parline's lawn, a hydrangea here, a peony there, a tiger lily beyond, in spaded spots of brown, mulch-filled earth, like so many chickens squatting in their round nests.

The Parlines were of English extraction although both had been born in Vermont. There was a faintly whispered tale that they were cousins, but there was no one so intimate as to verify the gossip and no one so prying as to ask.

Mr. Parline was a half head shorter than his tall, slender wife. He was stocky of body, a little ruddy as to complexion, like the color of his apples, a little fuzzy as to face, like the down on his peaches. There was a quiet dignity about him that fell just short of pompousness. "Mr. Parline" his wife called him, in contrast to the "John" and "Silas" and "Fred" with which the other women spoke of their liege lords. Where other women in the block ran into our home with the freedom of close acquaintances, Mrs. Parline alone occasionally came sedately in at the front gate in a neat brown dress covered with a large snowy apron starched to cardboard stiffness.

It was Mr. Parline who came often. With that manner which was paradoxically gentle and pompous, he would bring us edibles from his garden all summer long on a home-made flat wooden tray. That garden, as neat as constant care could make it, was the delight and despair of every one who attempted to emulate it. Not a pigweed showed its stubborn head. Not a mullein stalk lifted its thick velvety self. The bricklaid paths, without sign of leaf, might have been swept, even scrubbed. As for the growing contents of the garden, they made a varicolored and delightful picture. In its perfection every cabbage might have been a rose, every beet an exotic tropical plant, the parsley dainty window-box ferns. To Mr. Parline there was no dividing line between the beauty of flowers and the beauty of vegetables. With impartiality he planted marigolds near the carrots and zinnias next to the beans.

"Just a little of the fruits of my labor," was his

dignified greeting on those occasions when he tapped at the back door. In the center of the wooden tray might repose a cabbage, the dew still trembling upon the silver sheen of its leaves, around it a lovely mass of the delicate shell-pink of sweet peas. One felt it as much of a sacrilege to plunge the cabbage into hot water as it would have been to cook the sweet peas. Or, he might have several bunches of grapes in merging shades of wine-red and purple, their colors melting into the wine-red and purple colors of shaggy asters. Old Mr. Parline had the heart of a poet and the eye of an interior decorator.

We never saw Mrs. Parline pulling a vegetable or cutting a flower. Occasionally, at evening, she walked in the paths with all the interest and curiosity of a stranger, evidently considering the garden as sacred ground as did the rest of us. Indeed, Mother was at their back door one day when Mr. Parline came up the path with the inevitable wooden tray. There were beets on the tray, their tops cut, their bodies like blood-red hearts, around them white Sweet Williams and crimson phlox. "I was just bringing my wife some of the fruits of my labor," he said in his courteous, half-pompous way.

We laughed about the phrase at home. Ours was a noisy, hilarious, fun-loving family. One member might bring in a mess of dirty potatoes in a battered old pail. "A little of the fruits of my labor," he would imitate Mr. Parline's pompous dignity. Or another, coming in with the first scrawny radishes, might have placed a few limpsy dandelions around them as a floral satire on the contents of Mr. Parline's wooden tray.

If the garden was the old man's hobby, the weather was his very life. It was inconceivable that any one should be so wrapped up in the constant change of the elements. To other busy people the weather was incidental to their labors, the setting in which they performed their tasks. It might be pleasant or inconvenient, but it remained a side issue. To old Mr. Parline it was the important event of the day. He scanned the heavens, read the almanac, watched for signs of changes. Of the last he had a thousand at his command. If the sun went down in clouds on Friday night, if it rained the first Sunday in the month, if a dog ate grass, if the snow stuck to the north sides of the trees—he knew to a nicety what the results would be. To old Mr. Parline the weather was not the background.

It was the picture itself. It was not the mere setting for daily living. It was life itself. No government official connected with the Weather Bureau made it more his life's thought. In the kitchen he kept a large calendar upon which he made notations for the day. Every vagrant shifting of the wind, every cloud that raced across the blue was recorded. For what purpose no one knew. *Another slight dash of snow at noon. Temperature 34. Sun came out at 3* P.M. It seemed so small, so trivial, that a man should give so much time and thought to that which he could not change. He had thermometers by the house, on the north side to show the coldest registration, on the south to get the hottest, in the garden, by the barn. They were like traps everywhere—baited with mercury—little traps to catch the weather.

From Mr. Parline's conversation one gathered that an overseeing Providence had given him exclusive charge of the elements. If his words did not utter it, his manner implied it. "Well, how do you like my June day?" his attitude seemed to be. If the day was bad, he was half apologetic. If it was pleasant, he glowed with satisfaction. The summer afternoon on which we were to have a little social gathering, he came to the back door and with genuine feeling told us how sorry he was that the day was dull and rainy. His manner showed humiliation, as though from the standpoint of neighborliness he had failed us in a crisis. "I am very sorry," he said in his gentle, half-pompous way. "I had thought—had every reason to believe—that it would be sunshiny." We assured him that we bore him no grudge, and he went home relieved, returning with the wooden tray on which lay a heap of ruby cherries, a delicate mass of baby's-breath around them.

Was there a great national event, his talk turned immediately to the weather in which it was consummated. When he read the newspapers he seemed to ignore the main issue of the news. The weather, lurking in the background, was apparently of greater importance to him than the magnitude of the event. On the day of Admiral Dewey's triumph, he spoke immediately of the weather, wondering whether it had been dull or sunny in the harbor. At an inauguration there was no comment from him concerning the great issue of the day, the change in the policy of the Administration. He gave forth no acclaim or condemnation of the new head of the Government. His mind dwelt only on the fact that the new President was having to ride up Pennsylvania Avenue in a mist.

Vegetables, flowers, and the weather—they were Mr. Parline's whole existence. Such little things they were, we said. Whether his wife was bored by the triviality of his life, we could not know. She was too reserved for any one to sense her reactions to her husband's small interests. We could see her working about the house all day. Sometimes she brought out quilts and hung them on the line for cleaning. They were of intricate patterns, beautifully pieced and quilted —the Rose of Sharon, the Log Cabin, the Flower Basket, and the Rising Sun. "I'll bet the old man sleeps under the Rising Sun," one of the family remarked and we laughed uproariously at the joke. In the evening Mrs. Parline often came out and strolled through the paths, stepping gingerly about like a stranger, listening to the old man's courteous, half-pompous talk. She was deeply afraid of storms, he had told us years before. And when one saw the first dark clouds looming up from the southwest in summer, or the first gray ones rolling in from the north in winter, one also saw old Mr. Parline hurrying home, his square, heavy body swinging along out of its accustomed slower movements. To get home to

Mrs. Parline when there was rain or hail or snow was his first duty. It was the only time when he ever seemed thrown out of his pompous calm. You saw them later through the windows looking out at the storm together.

The Parlines attended a little ivy-grown church where the old gentleman passed the collection box. When his own part of the service was over he would take a seat near the door, one eye on the sky. It was as though he must have everything as auspicious as possible when the congregation should return home. One wondered if he heard the sermon at all. A queer old man.

But the queerest thing of all was his strange prophecy that the day would come when the weather could be regulated. We young folks guffawed at that. "He was eccentric before he sprung that one," we said, "but now he's a nut."

In his half-pompous, half-gentle way, he argued it. "In the centuries to come, who knows but that humanity will have progressed to such an extent that men can catch the weather and retain it—hold it for a time to their own choice? You smile at that." He was sensitive to our thoughts. "But strange things have happened. Who would have thought you could catch the human voice in a little box and listen to it through a tube to the ear?" This was all many years ago. "Who would have thought a machine would rise up in the air under its own power? Who would have thought carriages without horses would go about the streets?"

"The whole trouble would be," we joked with him, "you would want rain the day we wanted sunshine, and living next door to us, there would be complications."

"I don't pretend to know how it could be accomplished," he said in his gentle, dignified way. "I merely suggest that in the years to come it may be so."

So the Parlines went on living their quiet lives. Refined, gentle folk, but different—and a little queer.

And then on a spring day, old Mrs. Parline died, as quietly and unostentatiously as she had lived. There was no fuss about it. A hard cold, the doctor coming and going, a neighbor slipping in and out of the back door, a cousin coming out from Chicago to care for her—death. The various members of our family went over to the house. Other neighbors came, as they do in small towns. A man's sorrow is the town's sorrow. In a neighborly community, sympathy takes concrete form. It becomes buns and flowers and apple jelly and sitting up.

Old Mr. Parline greeted us kindly, courteously. Outwardly he showed no manifestations of his grief, except that his face was gray and drawn. He was solicitous of our comfort. He brought in fuel for the kitchen stove and oil for the lamps. He went to the cellar and came back with apples, polishing them scrupulously. He asked us if we were too cool or too hot. He went up and down the tulip beds pulling a few tiny weeds from the soil. Such little things in the face of death! He looked at the thermometer, at the almanac, at the sky, and predicted a pleasant, sunshiny afternoon for the services. A queer old man, we all said. Not even death itself could take his mind away from the habits of a lifetime.

Mrs. Parline was buried in Riverside Cemetery. "It seemed very mild out there this afternoon," he said to us a day or two after the services. "There was a light breeze from the northeast." We knew where "out there" was.

By Memorial Day there was a stone at the grave and a mass of scarlet geraniums which he had transplanted, and some parsley. "How odd," we said, "parsley from the vegetable garden."

But he was always odd. We walked around the stone to read the inscription. Propped up against it, in the lush grass, was a thermometer. We laughed a little—but only a little. Some laughter is half tears.

During that summer he seemed lost, a boat without a rudder. It was pathetic the way he went about his housework. He hung the quilts out on the line to clean them—the Flower Basket and the Log Cabin, the Rose of Sharon and the Rising Sun. We would see him, walking about the yard in the evening with a lantern, reading the thermometers.

"Look at that," we young folks said, "he's batty."

"Oh, no," Mother said, "he's lonely."

And then, quite suddenly, we realized that he was going out to the cemetery at the sign of every storm. At the first glimpse of a thunder-head looming up over the trees, we would see him slipping out of the white picket gate and hurrying down the street. In some indefinable way he must have felt that he wanted to carry out that old habit of protecting her.

"It's ridiculous," we said.

"It's beautiful," Mother said.

If we expected his garden to deteriorate, we

were mistaken. He took more pains with it than ever. More often he came to the back door with its products for us. Once, some one spoke tactfully about paying him, that he ought to have some compensation for his work. He looked pained. "Oh, no," he said, with gentle dignity. "Please do not speak of it again."

He found out the neighbors' various likes and dislikes. "I put out some turnips for you," he said to Mother. "I do not care for them myself, but I want you to have some." Yes, a kind old man.

And he continued to manage the weather. "I do not want to intrude." He came to the back door. "But I see your family is making preparations to go to a picnic."

"Yes, Mr. Parline. Wouldn't you like to go with us?"

"Oh, no, thank you. You are very kind. But I have work in my garden. I went to a picnic once in my youth. It was a very enjoyable occasion. I wanted to tell you that I think it will rain before night. The wind has switched to the east and the temperature is five degrees higher." The queer old codger.

And then, as the years went by, he began to include others than the immediate neighborhood in his gifts—people he had not known before and with whom he became acquainted in the cemetery.

A cemetery is a friendly place. You talk with people there whom you have not known in town. "The grass ought to be mowed," you may say to the wealthy widow by her husband's mausoleum, or "Do you think the peonies will be out by Memorial Day?" to the Italian fruit vendor by his baby's grave. So people who talked to the old man "out there," even though they lived across town, became the recipients of his garden products.

It was the day before Christmas in that third winter after his wife's death that the gray clouds of the big snow began rolling up from the northwest. Some one saw him slip out of his gate, lantern and green wreath in hand, and hurry down the street.

"You don't suppose that poor old man is going out there to the cemetery?" Mother was solicitous. She put a shawl over her head and hurried out a side door. We could hear her calling, "Oh, Mr. Parline!" When she came in she had deep sympathy in her eyes. "I told him I thought he ought not to go out when it looked so snowy. He said in his dignified old way, 'That's why I want to go. I must get out for a few minutes before the storm breaks.' I suppose he feels that he protects her just as he used to. Isn't it pathetic?"

We had our usual Christmas Eve oyster supper. Company came. It began to snow—soft, damp, heavy flakes. It was late when it came to us that there was no light in the Parline cottage. Father went over. When he found no one, he went after two other neighbors and together they went "out there." I think from the first they expected to find—what they found. He was huddled up against the stone where he had crumpled while stooping down to look at the thermometer. The doctor said death had been instantaneous, that he evidently had taxed himself hurrying to make the trip before the storm broke.

They brought him home. Neighbors went into the little house, not so immaculate as in the old days, but in order. In the kitchen they talked in low tones about the old man, as though from the front room where he lay he might hear their comments.

A queer old man, they all agreed, but kind, unusually kind. Mother went into the cellar and

brought up scarlet-cheeked apples and mellow pears.

"He would have wanted to pass them around," she said, with that understanding of humanity which she always seemed to possess. Scrupulously she polished them before she served them.

The cousin and a young married daughter came the day after Christmas. The cousin cried a little, tears that were not especially sad. "I didn't feel that I knew him very well," she told us. "When I took care of Cousin Sarah he was always very kind to me. He brought me everything from the garden and kept me supplied with fuel. But I never really got acquainted with him. When we did talk it seemed to be only about the weather. But he was a good old man."

They took him "out there" where his wife was, and the dead geraniums under their thick covering of snow, the green Christmas wreath, the parsley from the vegetable garden, and the thermometer.

The rest of the week it snowed and sleeted intermittently. On New Year's Eve, Mother and I went over and sat awhile with the cousin and her daughter. They replenished the fire in the kitchen stove with some of the wood Mr. Parline had brought in. They brought walnuts and jugs of cider from the cellar. The house had the lonely feeling that hangs over one from which a soul recently has gone.

Drawn by thoughts of the old man's hobby, Mother walked over to the huge bank calendar hanging there on the kitchen wall. The last day of the year it was, and so the last of the calendar with its few vacant pages. Mother thumbed over the last of the written ones, each filled with the old man's wavering writing. "Indications of snow. Wind in the east. Temperature 20 at the north side of the house, 19 at the barn, 18 out there." Underneath was a homemade set of shelves, all the old calendars of bygone years in neat piles, the dates printed on the backs.

Through the clean, small-paned window, we could see low clouds breaking and slipping into the east. We were no doubt thinking the same thought—of the old man lying "out there" in the dignity of death, with the scudding clouds and the wind in the west, the old man who had lived close to the wind and the rain, the hail and the snow. Death would not seem so significant to him tonight as the importance of the setting —the rift in the clouds and the end of the storm.

There was the last of the few vacant pages on

the calendar. He would have wanted it filled. Mother looked at it for a moment, then picked up the short, stubby pencil hanging limply on its long string, and wrote the weather for the day—the gentle old man's long Day: *Shadows gone from the valley—no night—and the need of no candle—sunshine—eternal sunshine—and the Seven Stars.*

Bid the Tapers Twinkle

THE Atkin house sat well back in a tree-filled yard on a busy corner of town, its wide frame porch running around two sides, thirty feet of it facing Churchill Avenue, thirty feet facing Seventh Street, its long brick walk sloping across the lot to an iron gateway in the exact corner, as though with impartial deference to both streets.

The arrangement might have been almost symbolic of the character of old Mrs. Atkin, who had lived there for many years, so impartially gracious to her well-to-do Churchill Avenue callers and her hired help from Seventh Street.

Old Sara Atkin had known the town longer than any one now living in it. Indeed, she had arrived as a bride only a few weeks after the first timbers were laid for the sawmill which became the nucleus of a village. She had seen a store go up near the sawmill, a single pine room with a porch across the front, onto which a man threw a sack of mail from the back of a pony twice a week. She had seen the first house built—a queer little box of a cottonwood house; had seen another follow, and others; then a one-roomed school-house and a stout frame church with a thick spire like a work-worn hand pointing a clumsy finger to the blue sky. She had seen whips of cottonwood trees set out at the edge of the grassy streets, had watched them grow to giants, live out their lives and fall to the ground under the axes of the third generation. She had seen a shining roadway of steel laid through the village and the first iron horse snort its way into the sunset. All these things and many others had old Sara Atkin seen.

John Atkin had gone back to Ohio for her and brought her by wagon and ferry to his bachelor sod house on land he had purchased from the railroad company for two dollars an acre. She had been nineteen then, her cheeks as pink as the wild roses that sprang up in the prairie grass, her eyes as blue as the wild gentians that grew near them.

A few years later they had moved into a new three-room house with a lean-to and turned the soddie over to the stock. John Atkin had possessed the knack of making money where some of his neighbors had not. He had started a general store and a sorghum mill, had shipped in coal and lumber, had prospered to such an extent in a short time, that they were able to build the present residence, a castle of a house for the raw prairie town—so unusual, with its parlor and back parlor and its two fireplaces, that people had driven for miles in their top buggies or buckboards to see its capacious framework and the mottled marble of its mantels.

When it was completed, new furniture had come for it too—walnut bedsteads and center tables and a tall hall rack with a beveled-glass mirror. But the house which had once been such a source of pride to the whole community was merely a fussy and rather shabby old place now, with its furniture outmoded. John Atkin had been dead for many years, and Sara, whose cheeks had once been like wild roses, was a great-grandmother.

In the passing years the town had taken on an unbelievable size, and even a bit of sophistication, with its fine homes and university, its business blocks and country clubs. It had grown noisily around Sara Atkin; the tide of traffic now banged and clanged on the paved corner that had once been rutty and grass-grown.

But even though a filling station had gone up

across the alley on the Seventh Street side and rather high-priced apartments on the Churchill Avenue side, old Sara would not leave, but stayed on in the fussy house with the walnut hall rack and the marble mantels.

She lived there all alone, too, except for the daily presence of one Jennie Williams, who came ploddingly down Seventh Street each day to work. Once, in Jennie's high-school days, Sara had taken her on temporarily until she could find someone else to help. But Jennie had grown fat and forty waiting for Mrs. Atkin to find another girl.

This morning she came puffingly through the kitchen door in time to see Sara Atkin turning the page of the drug-store calendar on the kitchen wall and pinning back the flapping leaf so that the word "December" stood out boldly.

Old Sara greeted Jennie with a subtle, "Do you know what date this is, Jennie?"

She asked the same darkly mysterious question every year, and, as always, Jennie feigned surprise: "Don't tell me it's December a'ready, Mis' Atkin?"

Yes, it was December; old Sara Atkin's own special month—the one for which she lived, the one toward which all the other months led like steps to some shining Taj Mahal. It was the month in which all the children came home.

"It's true, Jennie. Time again to bid the tapers twinkle fair. Did I ever tell you how our family came to use that expression, Jennie?"

Jennie had heard the explanation every year for a quarter of a century, but she obligingly assumed ignorance.

"How's that, Mis' Atkin?" As a stooge Jennie Williams could not have been surpassed.

Sara Atkin's white old face took on a glow. "Well, it was years ago. My goodness, I don't know how many—maybe forty-one or two; I could figure it out if I took time. But our Dickie was just a little chap—that's Mr. Richard Atkin, you know, my lawyer son—and he was going to speak his first piece in the new schoolhouse on Christmas Eve. The piece he was to give began:

"We hang up garlands everywhere
And bid the tapers twinkle fair.

"When you stop to think about it, Jennie, that's a hard line for anybody to say, let alone a little codger with his first piece. I can just see him—he had on a little brown suit I'd made him and was so round and roly-poly, and he stood up so bravely in front of all of those folks and began so cute:

> " 'We hang up garlands everywhere
> And bid the twapers tinkle tair.' "

"He knew something was wrong—every one was grinning—and he stopped and tried again, but this time he got it:

> " 'And bid the taters pinkle tair.' "

"Every one laughed out loud and he said, 'I mean:

> " 'And tid the bapers finkle fair.' " "

Sara Atkin laughed at the little memory so dear to her old heart, and Jennie politely followed suit with as extensive a show of hilarity as one could muster after hearing the anecdote for twenty-five years.

"Richard never heard the last of it. And after that whenever Christmas was coming we'd always say it was time to bid the tapers twinkle fair. I guess all big families have jokes that way, Jennie."

"I guess yours more than most folks, Mis' Atkin. My, I never knew anybody to make such a hullabaloo over Christmas as you Atkinses do."

It was just faintly possible that a bit of acidity had crept into Jennie's voice. The coming month was not going to be exactly a period of inertia for fat, slow Jennie. But to old Sara it was merely an invitation to indulge in a line of reminiscences, so that it was almost a half hour before Jennie needed to start working.

Jennie Williams was right. The Atkins made much of Christmas festivities.

There are those to whom Christmas means little or nothing; those whose liking for it is more or less superficial; those who worship it with a love that cannot be told. Sara Atkin had always been one of these last. Christmas to her meant the climax of the year, the day for which one lived. It meant vast preparation, the coming together of the clan. She had never been able to understand women to whom it was merely half interesting, sometimes even a cause for complaint. From the first Christmas in the sod house with a makeshift tree for the baby to the previous year with twenty-one coming, she had sunk herself in loving preparation for the day. No matter what experiences had preceded it— drought, blizzards, crop failures, financial losses, illness—she had approached The Day with a warmth of gladness, an uplift of the spirit which no other season could bring forth.

In those old pioneer days she had neighbors who possessed no initiative by which to make Christmas gifts out of their meager supplies. She herself had known that it took only love and energy to make them.

There had been two sons and two daughters born to her. They were middle-aged now, but by some strange magic she had transmitted to them this vital love for the Christmastime, so that they, too, held the same intense ardor for the day. In the years that were gone sons and grandsons had wrangled with wives that they must go to Grandma Atkin's for Christmas. As for the daughters and granddaughters, they had made it clear from the times of their engagements that it was not even a subject for debate whether they should attend the family reunion. To the Atkin descendants at large old Sara Atkin *was* Christmas.

So now the annual preparations began. Life took on a rose-colored hue for old Sara, and a dark blue one for Jennie. Rugs came out to be beaten and curtains down to be washed. Permanent beds were made immaculate and temporary ones installed. A dozen cook-books were consulted and the tree ordered. Jennie in her obesity and obstinacy was urged gently to try to make more effective motions. Once in her happiness old Sara said chucklingly:

"Jennie, Doctor Pitkin was wrong. Life begins at eighty."

To which Jennie made acrid reply, "Good land, don't tell me you've took up with a new doctor at your age, Mis' Atkin."

Eva, dropping in from a bridge afternoon, found her mother on the couch at the close of a day's preparations, a pan of strung pop corn at her side. The daughter was perturbed, scolded a little.

"Mother, what is there about you that makes you attack Christmas this hard way? You'll make yourself sick. Why don't we all go to the University Club? We can get a private room if we get in our bid right away."

"What—a club? On Christmas? Not while I have a roof over my head."

"But you do so many unnecessary things. No one strings pop corn any more for a tree. That was in the days when there weren't so many decorations."

"There's no law against it," said old Sara.

"Or is there," she twinkled, "since the government has so much to say?"

In a few days Eva dropped in again. She had
something on her mind, was hesitant in getting
it out, averted her eyes a bit when she told it.
"Mother, I hope I'm not going to disappoint
you too much, but Fred and I think our family
will have to go to Josephine's for Christmas.
She's the farthest away . . . and can't come . . .
and would like to have us . . . and . . ." Her voice
trailed off apologetically.

Old Sara was sorry. But, "You do what's best,"
she said cheerily. She must not be selfish. It was
not always possible for all of them to be with
her, so she would not let it disturb her.

She told Jennie about it next morning.
"There will be five less than we thought, Jennie.
My daughter, Mrs. Fleming, and Professor
Fleming and their daughter's family won't be
here."

Jennie was not thrown into a state which one
might term brokenhearted, interpreting the
guests' attendance as she did in terms of food
and dishes.

The next evening Sara Atkin had a long-distance call from Arnold. He visited with his
mother with alarming lack of toll economy—in

fact, it was some little time before he led up to
the news that they were not coming. He and
Mame and the boys were going to Marian's.
Marian's baby was only nine months old and
Marian thought it better for them all to come
there.

When she assured him it was all right old Sara
tried her best to keep a quaver out of her voice.
In her disappointment she did not sleep well.
In the morning she broke the news to Jennie
with some slight manipulating of the truth, in-
asmuch as she told her there was a faint possi-
bility that not all of Arnold's family might get
there.

When the letter from Helen arrived next day
she had almost a premonition, so that her eyes
went immediately down the page to the distressing statement. They were not coming. They
couldn't afford it this year, Helen said—not after
the drought. It hurt Sara worse than the others.
It wasn't a reason. It was an excuse. That wasn't
true about not affording it. It had been a bad
year of drought, but Carl had his corn loan. If
she had died they could have afforded to come
to the funeral. And she could not bring herself
to tell Jennie they, too, were not coming. She
had too much pride to let Jennie know that

Helen and Carl, who had no children to provide for or educate, thought they were too poor to come home for Christmas.

She had scarcely laid the letter and her glasses aside when the phone rang. It was Mr. Schloss telling her that the turkeys were in. "I'll save you two as always, Mis' Atkin?"

"Yes," said old Sara. Two turkeys for no one but herself and Richard and Clarice and their son Jimmie, who was sixteen. But she would not admit that the Atkin reunion was to be composed of only four people.

Before breakfast the next morning the night letter came in:

SORRY CAN'T COME MOTHER STOP JIMMIE HAS HARD COLD CAUGHT IT PLAYING BASKETBALL STOP HOPE MESSAGE DOESN'T FRIGHTEN YOU STOP THOUGHT LET YOU KNOW RIGHT AWAY STOP SENDING PACKAGES STOP WILL BE THINKING OF YOU ALL DAY CHRISTMAS

RICHARD

Old Sara got up and shut the door between herself and the kitchen, for fear that Jennie would come in and see her before she had gained control of herself. Twenty-one of them.

And not one was coming. It was unbelievable. She sat stunned, the telegram still in her hand. She tried to reason with herself, but she seemed to have no reasoning powers; tried to comfort herself, but the heart had gone out of her. All her life she had held to a philosophy of helpfulness, but she knew now she was seeing herself as she really was. A great many people who had no relatives for Christmas gatherings made it a point to invite those who were lonely. They went out into the highways and hedges and brought them in. The Bible said to do so. Old Sara didn't want to. Tears filled her old eyes. She didn't want lonely people from the highways and hedges. She wanted her own folks. *She wanted all the Atkins.*

Jennie was at work in the kitchen now. She seemed slower than ever this morning, trudging about heavily in her flat-heeled slippers. Sara did not care, did not hurry her, gave her no extra duties.

The morning half over, the phone rang, and it was Mr. Schloss again. "Ve got de trees dis mornin', Mis' Atkin. Fine nice vons. I tell you first so you can get your choice same as always. Can you come over?"

Jennie was listening, craning her head to

hear. Something made old Sara do it. "Yes, I'll come over."

Mr. Schloss led her mysteriously through the store to the back. "I like you to get the pick. Folks all comin', I suppose? I never saw such relations as you got to have dose goot Christmases. Like when I'm a boy in Germany. Most folks now, it ain't so much to dem any more."

He sent the tree right over by a boy. Sara and Jennie had the big pail ready with the wet gravel in it. The boy told them Mr. Schloss said he was to stay and put it up. They placed it in the front parlor by the mottled marble fireplace, its slender green tip reaching nearly to the ceiling. Jennie got down the boxes of ornaments and tinsels and placed them invitingly on the mantel. Old Sara started to decorate. She draped and festooned and stood back mechanically to get the effect, her old eyes not seeing anything but her children, her ears not hearing anything but silence louder than ever noise had been.

For the next two days she went on mechanically with preparations. Before Christmas Eve she would rouse herself and ask in some people —the food and decorations must not be wasted. She would probably have Grandma Bremmer and her old-maid daughters. They would be glad to get the home cooking, but Christmas had never meant very much to them. It was just another day at the hotel. Not a vital thing. Not a warm, living experience. Not a fundamental necessity, as it was to the Atkins.

In the meantime her pride would not allow her to tell Jennie or the merchants or the occasional caller who dropped in. "Our family reunion is to be cut down quite a bit this year," she would say casually. "Some of them aren't coming."

Some? Not one was coming.

In the late afternoon before Christmas Eve snowflakes began falling, as lazily as though fat Jennie were scattering them. The house was immaculate, everything prepared.

"Shall I put all the table leaves in, Mis' Atkin?" Jennie was asking.

"No," said Old Sara. "You needn't stay to set the table at all. The—the ones that get here will be in time to help."

"I've got a package I'm bringing you in the morning," Jennie informed her.

"So have I one for you, Jennie. Come early . . . we . . . we'll open them by the tree."

"Well, good night then, Mis' Atkin, and Merry Christmas."

"Good night, Jennie—and Merry Christmas."

Jennie was gone and the house was quiet. The snowflakes were falling faster. The house was shining from front to back. Beds were ready. The tree was sparkling with colored lights, packages from all the children under its tinseled branches. The cupboards were filled with good food. So far as preparations were concerned, everything was ready for the family reunion. And no one but herself knew that there was to be no reunion.

Later in the evening she would call up the Bremmers. But in the meantime she would lie down in the back parlor and rest. Strange how very tired she felt, when there had been so little confusion. She pulled a shawl about her and lay down on the old leather couch.

Through the archway she could see the tree, shining in all its bravery, as though trying to be gay and gallant. Then she nodded and it looked far away and small. She dozed, awakened, dozed again. The tiny tree out there now had tufts of cotton from a quilt on it, bits of tinfoil from a package of tea, homemade candles of mutton tallow. It was a queer little cottonwood tree trying to look like an evergreen—a tree such as she had in the pioneer days.

She could not have told the exact moment in which she began to hear them, could not have named the precise time in which she first saw them vaguely through the shadows. But somewhere on the borderland of her consciousness she suddenly realized they were out there under the crude little tree. Arnold was examining a homemade sled, his face alight with boyish eagerness. Eva and Helen were excitedly taking the brown paper wrappings from rag dolls. Dickie was on the floor spinning a top made from empty spools. Every little face was clear, every little figure plain. For a long time she watched them playing under the makeshift tree, a warm glow of happiness suffusing her whole being. Some vague previous hurt she had experienced was healed. Everything was all right. The children were here.

Then she roused, swept her hand over her eyes in the perplexity of her bewilderment, felt herself grow cold and numb with the disappointment of it. The children were not here. When you grew old you must face the fact that you could have them only in dreams.

It was almost dusk outside now, with the falling of the early December twilight. Christmas Eve was descending—the magic hour before the coming of the Child. It was the enchanted time in which all children should seek their homes— the family time. So under the spell of the magic moment was she that when the bell rang and she realized it was not the children, she thought at first that she would not pay any attention to the noisy summons. It would be some kind friend or neighbor whose very kindness would unnerve her. But the habit of years was strong. When one's bell rang, one went to the door.

So she rose, brushed back a straying lock, pulled her wool shawl about her shoulders and went into the hallway, holding her head gallantly.

"Merry Christmas, mother. . . . Merry Christmas, grandma." It came from countless throats, lustily, joyfully.

"Bid the tapers twinkle fair, mother."

"He means bid the taters finkle tair, grandma." Laughter rose noisily.

She could not believe it. Her brain was addled. The vision of the children under the tree had been bright, also. This was another illusion.

But if the figures on the porch were wraiths from some hinterland they were very substantial ones. If they were apparitions they were then phantoms which wore fur coats and tweeds and knitted sport suits, shadows whose frosty breath came forth in a most unghostly fashion in the cold air of the December twilight.

They were bursting through the doorway now, bringing mingled odors of frost, holly, faint perfumes, food, mistletoe, evergreens; stamping snow from shoes, carrying packages to the chins—Eva and Fred, Arnold and Mame, Dick and Clarice, Helen and Carl, Josephine and her family, Marian with her husband and baby, Richard's Jimmie, and Arnold's boys. They noisily filled the old hall, oozed out into the dining-room, backed up the stairway, fell over the tall old walnut hatrack. They did not once cease their loud and merry talking.

"Aren't we the rabble?"

"Did you ever know there were so many Atkins?"

"We look like a movie mob scene."

"The President should give us a silver loving cup or something."

They surged around old Sara Atkin, who had her hand on her throat to stop the tumultuous beating of its pulse.

"But I don't understand. Why did—why did

you say you weren't coming?" she was asking feebly of those nearest to her.

Several feminine voices answered simultaneously—Eva and Helen and Dick's wife. "To save you working your fingers to the bone, mother. The way you always slave—it's just ridiculous."

"We decided that the only way to keep you from it was just to say we weren't any of us coming, and then walk in the last minute and bring all the things."

"Carl and I couldn't think of an excuse." It was Helen. "So we laid it to the poor old drought. And we'd a perfectly dreadful time— writing and phoning around to get it planned, what every one should do. I brought the turkey all ready for the oven. . . . Carl, where's the turkey? Get it from the car."

"Fred and I have the tree outside and——" Eva broke off to say, "Why, mother, *you've* a tree?"

Clarice said, "Oh, look, folks, her packages are under it. And she thought she was going to open them all by herself. Why that makes me feel teary."

Old Sara Atkin sat down heavily in a hall chair. There were twenty-one of them—some of them flesh of her flesh. They had done this for her own good, they thought. Twenty-one of them—and not one had understood how much less painful it is to be tired in your body than to be weary in your mind—how much less distressing it is to have an ache in your bones than to have a hurt in your heart.

There was the oyster supper, gay and noisy. There were stockings hung up and additional Christmas wreaths. There was Christmas music from a radio and from a phonograph and from the more-or-less unmusical throats of a dozen Atkins. There were Christmas stories and Christmas jokes. There were wide-eyed children put to bed and a session of grown people around the tree. There were early lights on Christmas morning and a great crowd of Atkins piling out in the cold of their bedrooms and calling raucous Merry Christmases to one another. There was a hasty unwanted breakfast with many pert remarks about hurrying up. There was the great family circle about the fireplace and the tree with Arnold Atkin, Jr., calling out the names on the gifts, accompanied by a run of funny flippances. There were snow banks of tissue paper and entanglements of string. There was the turkey dinner. And through it all, after the manner of the Atkin clan, there was constant talk and laughter.

The noise beat against the contented mind of Sara Atkin all day, like the wash of breakers against the sturdy shore.

All of this transpired until the late Christmas afternoon, when the entire crowd went up to Eva's new home near the campus.

"Don't you feel like coming, too, mother?"

"No, I'm a little tired and I'll just rest awhile before you come back."

They were gone. The house was appallingly quiet after the din of the passing day. There was no sound but the pad-padding of Jennie Williams in the kitchen.

Old Sara lay down on the couch in the back parlor. Through the archway she could see a portion of the disheveled front room, over which a cyclone apparently had swept. The tree with its lights still shining gaily stood in the midst of the débris.

In her bodily weariness she nodded, dozed, awakened, dozed. Suddenly the tree blurred, then grew enormous; the green of its branches became other trees, a vast number of them springing from the shadows. They massed together in a huge cedar forest, some candle laden and some electric lighted, but all gallant with Christmas cheer. Under the branches were countless children and grown people. And then suddenly she almost laughed aloud, to see that they were all her own. There were a dozen Arnolds, a dozen Helens—all her boys and girls at all their ages playing under all the trees which had ever been trimmed for them. It was as though in one short moment she had seen together the entire Christmases of the sixty years.

She roused and smiled at the memory of having seen such a wondrous sight. "Well, I suppose there'll not be many more for me," she thought, "but I've passed on the tapers. They all love it as I do. They won't forget to light the tapers after—after I'm gone."

Then she sat up and threw off her shawl with vehement gesture. "Fiddlesticks! Imagine me talking that way about dying—as if I were an old woman. I'm only eighty-one. I'm good for a dozen more Christmases. My body isn't feeble —at least—only at times. As for my mind—my mind's just as clear as a bell."

She rose and went out to the dining-room. Jennie Williams was trudging about putting away the last of the best dishes. Some of the women had helped her, but there were a dozen things she had been obliged to finish herself. She was tired and cross with the unnecessary work and the undue commotion. Her feet hurt her. She liked the peaceful, slow days better.

"Well, Jennie, it's all over," old Sara said happily. "We had a good time, same as always. We've had a grand day to bid the tapers twinkle fair. Jennie, did I ever tell you how we Atkins happened to start using that expression?"

Jennie jerked her heavy body about and opened her mouth to answer determinedly, for she felt her provocation was great. But she stopped suddenly at the sight of old Sara Atkin standing in the doorway. For old Sara's sweet white face glowed with an inner light, and the illumination from the tree behind her gave the appearance of a halo around her head. Suddenly Jennie Williams had a strange thought about old Sara. It was that Mary the Mother might have looked that way when she was old.

"No," said Jennie kindly. "I don't believe you ever have told me, Mis' Atkins. How *did* you?"

Christmas On the Prairie

(*From* A Lantern In Her Hand)

E VERY one was in want that year of 1874. In the early fall people began going past the house. "Going home," they all reported. Many times parties of them stayed all night. They had their own quilts and would arrange their beds on the main-room floor. They were beaten, they said. One could stand a few disappointments and failures, but when everything turned against one, there was no use trying to fight.

"Nebraska hasn't turned against us," Will would argue stubbornly. "It's the finest, blackest land on the face of the earth. The folks that will just stick it out.... You'll see the climate change, ... more rains and not so much wind ... when the trees grow. We've got to keep at the trees. Some day this is going to be the richest state in the union ... the most productive. I'll bet anything next year ..."

Always "next year"! It was a mirage, thought Abbie, an apparition that vanished when one came to it. Six times now they had said, "Next year, the crops will be fine."

And so she could not throw off the blue mood that had descended upon her, a horde of worries that had come upon her even as the horde of grasshoppers had come upon the land. The thought that there was nothing to do with; that they could scarcely keep body and soul together; that she probably would never be able now to do anything with her voice; that another child was coming,—they all harassed and tormented her. All fall there was in her mind a tired disinterest over things. In spite of what he said, that surface courage which he pretended had returned to him, Abbie detected that Will, too, was morose. To her keen eye he seemed dull and stoical, underneath an assumption of cheerfulness.

Before cold weather, the old grasshoppers were gone, but first they had taken infinite pains to leave a reminder of themselves in the newly broken prairie everywhere,—holes the size of lead pencils in which they laid one to two dozen eggs in a sack. In a six-inch square of ground, Will testing their number, found a double handful of the next year's hatching. There seemed not even a hope for the following crop.

It was in November that the barrel and box came from the folks back home. Will drove up to the soddie with rattling announcement of their arrival. A letter from Grandpa Deal had been the forerunner of the donations and already Abbie knew that an old brass horn of Dennie's was among the things for Mack. She determined to slip it out without his knowledge and put it away for Christmas. They all gathered around the barrel while Will pried open the top, Mack and Margaret dancing about in an ecstasy of excitement. The first thing to be taken out was an envelope marked "For Abbie," in Grandpa Deal's handwriting. In it was twenty dollars. Abbie cried a little, tears of love and homesickness, happiness and relief, and put it away with secret thoughts of the desired organ. She sensed that Grandpa had slipped it in with his one hand the last thing, so Grandma would not see it.

There were flower seeds and sugar and beans, seed-corn and dried apples in the barrel. Mother Mackenzie had tied and sent two thick comforts. Regina Deal sent an old soiled white silk bonnet with a bead ornament and a cluster of three little pink feathers on it,—"tips," Abbie told the children they were,—and a pair of dirty white "stays" and some old white hoop-skirts. Abbie laughed until she cried at the sight of them.

"Maybe I could put the hoops over some stakes next summer and keep the setting hens in them," she suggested. She put them on over her work dress, the hoops and the stays both, and perched the dirty bonnet on her red-brown hair, dancing about in them, the three noble tips nodding with uncertain dignity as though, like their former owner, they had no sense of humor. She pushed Will and Mack and Margaret into position for a square dance and showed the children how to "whirl your partner" and "alamand left." The four of them pranced around in the impromptu dance, the children in their patched dingy clothing, Will in his denim work things, and Abbie in the foolish soiled cast-offs which Regina had sent with so little thought. The two older children laughed and clapped their hands and shouted that they had never had so much fun in their lives, and little John toddled in and out and between them in an ecstasy of bubbling spirits.

It broke something in Abbie, some tight-bound band around her heart and throat, which had not been loosed for months. She hid the old brass horn of Dennie's in the bedroom. She put away the precious dried apples and pop-corn, the seed-corn and the big solid Greenings from the orchard behind Grandpa Deal's house. She hugged the huge warm quilts as though they were the fat pudding-bag body of Maggie Mackenzie. The bad luck was temporary. They were young and well. The children were all healthy youngsters. Why, how wicked she had been! She was only twenty-seven. She mustn't let her voice rust the way she had done this summer. In another year or so she could have an organ and maybe even get to a music teacher. She mustn't let youth slip away and her voice go with it. She was ashamed of herself that she had not sung for months.

> "Oh! the Lady of the Lea,
>   Fair and young and gay was she."

Her voice rose full-throated, mellowed now with tribulations and sympathy. The children clapped their hands that Mother was singing.

> "Beautiful exceedingly,
>   The Lady of the Lea."

She replenished the fire of twisted hay and corn-cobs in the stove with the four holes and the iron hearth in front. She cooked cornmeal mush for supper and set the table. Several times she sang the same verses over.

"Many a wooer sought her hand,
   For she had gold and she had land,"

The teakettle sang and the children chattered happily at the window. She lighted the coal-oil lamp with the red flannel in the bowl and washed her hands in the tin basin. The prairie twilight came on. The winds died down.

"Everything at her command,
   The Lady of the Lea."

Will came in from doing the chores.
"It's the nicest time of day . . . isn't it, Will . . . the red fire of the corn . . . and the steaming teakettle . . . supper ready . . . and the children all alive and well . . . and you and I together?"
Will put his arm around her for a brief, rare moment.
"It's the nicest time of day, Abbie-girl."

Yes, the coming of the barrel seemed to put something back into Abbie which had been gone temporarily,—laughter and hope, courage and faith. She began planning right away for Christmas. Mack was nearly eight, Margaret six and little John two. They were going to have the finest Christmas they had ever known. To Abbie's pleasure, Will entered into the preparations, too. He was as glad to see Abbie come to life as she was to see him throw off a little of his moroseness.

She told Gus and Christine Reinmueller their plans.

"*Ach!*" Christine snorted. "So? *Gans närrish* . . . voolish."

"A heck of a Christmas we'll have," was Gus's equally enthusiastic response.

But Abbie found sympathy in Sarah Lutz,— Sarah, with her little black beady eyes and her cheerful, energetic way.

"You know, Sarah, I think every mother owes it to her children to give them happy times at Christmas. They'll remember them all their lives. I even think it will make better men and women of them."

"I think so, too, Abbie. We're going to have a cedar tree hauled up from the Platte. Henry can get you one, too."

All day long Abbie worked at the tasks that demanded attention, washing, ironing, patch-ing, mending, baking, churning, caring for the chickens,—all with meager equipment or no equipment at all. Two wooden tubs, three heavy, clumsy flat-irons, a churn with wooden dasher, scissors, needles and thread, and a baking board with a few heavy dishes and utensils. But from them, clean clothes, sweet butter, neatly made-over suits and dresses and food that was palatable. The tapering Mackenzie fingers were calloused and burned and pricked. As tired as all these tasks left her, she would get the children to bed early and then bring out the Christmas things and begin working on them.

She got out the precious paints Mrs. Whitman had given her and worked on a picture for Will when he was away. It was a scene of the prairie with a clump of cottonwoods in the foreground. She tried to get the afterglow of the sunset but even though she worked faithfully, she could not get it. "If I only had some one to help a little," she would say. "Some day I want to take some painting lessons again. If I could just make a picture as I want to,—it would satisfy something in me."

From the barn she got clean husks and made a family of dolls for Margaret. She made the bodies, heads and limbs from the husks and braided the corn-silk for hair. A man, a lady and a baby, she made, and dressed them in corn-husk clothes. Will built a small bedstead for them. Out of one of the coats in the barrel she made Mack a new suit and concocted a bonnet for Margaret out of the old one Regina had sent, trimming it with a little wisp of the pink tips. With her paints, she marked off a checkerboard for Mack, and Will whittled checkers from the circumference of some small cottonwood branches. She cut a pattern and made a calico dog for little John, stuffing it with corn-husks, and covering it with knotted ends of carpet rags to give it a woolly appearance. She ironed out brown wrapping paper, tied the pieces with yarn and drew waggish-looking cows and horses on it for him, too.

Margaret laboriously hemmed a handkerchief for her father and Mack made him a box for his newspapers. There was a State Journal now, and as scarce as money was, Will had subscribed. "We can't drop out of touch with other parts of the country," he had said. "And we must know what the rest of the settlers are doing."

The children could talk of nothing but the approach of the wonderful day. The word "he" had only one meaning in their vocabulary,—a portly gentleman with a white beard and a sack on his back.

"Are you sure he'll come this year, Mother? Heinie Reinmueller said he wouldn't. He said his mother said so."

"Of *course* he'll come," Abbie assured the three. "Because Father and I are making things, too, to help him when he comes."

With Scotch-Irish cleverness, she could think of a dozen things to do with her meager supplies to add to the festivities. She ran tallow in tiny molds for the candles. She made a little batch of molasses candy and baked cookies in star and diamond shapes. She boiled eggs and painted faces on them and made little calico bonnets for them.

Christine was contemptuous toward the unnecessary festivities.

"For dot ... no time I haf. You learn 'em vork ... cows milk 'n' pigs svill ... 'n' dey for foolishness no time haf."

"Oh, don't let us ever get like Reinmuellers," Abbie said. "We're poor. If we were any poorer we might as well lie down and give up. But we can fight to keep civilized... can fight to keep something before us besides the work."

On the day before Christmas the snow lay

deep on the prairie and the children's greatest anxiety was whether "he" would find the little house which was half buried. Margaret, with the characteristic ingenuity of the female of the species, suggested tying a piece of bright cloth where "he" would notice it. And Mack, with the characteristic daring of the less deadly of the same, got on top of the low house via a crusty snow bank and tied one of little John's red flannel shirts to the stove-pipe.

At lamp-lighting, they all hung up their stockings, even Will and Abbie. The children were beside themselves with excitement. By their parents' stockings they put the little presents they had made for them. They danced and skipped and sang. They cupped their eyes with their hands, pressing their faces to the little half-window and looking out into the night. The gleam of the stars was reflected in the snow, and the silence of the sky was the silence of the prairie.

"I see the Star."

"So do I. Right up there."

"It looks like it was over a stable."

"Yes, sir. It looks like it was over a manger-stable."

"Now it looks like it's stopping over us."

"Yes, sir, it looks like it's stopping right over *our* house."

Wide-eyed, they went to bed. The three faces in a row on the pillows, with the patchwork quilts tucked under the chins, were flushed with anticipation.

"Always keep the Christmas spirit going," Abbie told them. "Promise me, that when you get big and have homes of your own, you'll keep the Christmas spirit in your homes."

"We will," they promised in glib and solemn accord.

When at last they slept, Will brought in the little cedar tree. The morning found it trimmed with popcorn and tallow candles. And a marvelous flock of butterflies had settled upon it. Their bodies were of dried apples dipped in sugar and their antennæ were pink and feathery, looking surprisingly as though they had once adorned Regina Deal's bonnet. Will had made and painted Abbie a corner what-not with four shelves, secreting it in the stable behind some straw bedding. And he had constructed a monstrous hobby-horse for the children, the body and head of cottonwood chunks, real horse's hair for mane and tail, reins and a bit in the steed's cut-out mouth. The wooden horse of

Troy never looked so huge. And then the old brass horn was unwrapped.

"I'm so excited," Mack said, in solemn ecstasy. "I'm so excited . . . my legs itch."

Historians say, "The winter of 'seventy-four to 'seventy-five was a time of deep depression." But historians do not take little children into consideration. Deep depression? To three children on the prairie it was a time of glamour. There was not much to eat in the cupboard. There was little or no money in the father's flat old pocketbook. The presents were pitifully homely and meager. And all in a tiny house,— a mere shell of a house, on a new raw acreage of the wild, bleak prairie. How could a little rude cabin hold so much white magic? How could a little sod house know such enchantment? And how could a little hut like that eventually give to the midwest so many influential men and women? How, indeed? Unless, . . . unless, perchance, the star *did* stop over the house?

It was a half century later and Abbie made her usual extensive preparations for Christmas that year. The daughters and daughters-in-law said a great deal against her using up so much energy. "But you might as well talk to the wind," Grace wrote to Isabelle. "There's something stubborn about Mother. She is bound to go through with all that mincemeat, doughnut, pop-corn-ball ordeal even if she's sick in bed afterward. Margaret wants us to come there to save her all that work, and Emma and Eloise have both offered their homes, too, but she won't listen. 'No,' she says, 'as long as I'm here, the Christmas gathering is here.' I've tried to tell her over and over that conditions have changed, that we don't live out on an isolated prairie any more; that she doesn't make one thing that she couldn't buy, but she just won't catch up with the times. 'They're not so full of the Christmas spirit when you don't fix them yourself,' she says. Isn't that the last word in old-fashioned ideas?"

So the clan came once more to the old farmhouse behind the cedars. Grace was the first to arrive in her own roadster, coming over the graveled highway from Wesleyan University. The others arrived at various times before Christmas eve. Mack and Emma, Donald and Katherine came. Only Stanley was missing from the Mack Deal family. Having married, Stanley had discovered that a wife's people must also be reckoned with. Margaret and Dr. Fred Baker.

Dr. Fred, Jr., and his wife and two little boys came. Isabelle and Harrison Rhodes got in from Chicago on the afternoon train, the road boasting a flyer now instead of the old baggage-and-day affair of the time when the children were small. John and Eloise, Wentworth and Laura and Millard, who was eight now, all came over from their home on the other side of Cedartown in time for the evening meal. Every car was loaded to the doors with packages.

Abbie had an oyster supper. That, too, was a hang-over from the days when sea food was scarce and expensive. No matter that the bivalves were on every menu placed before the various members of the Deal family these days, Abbie continued to have an oyster supper each Christmas eve,—bowls of crackers alternating down the long table with celery, standing upright in vase-looking dishes, like so many bouquets from the greenhouse.

Jimmie Buchanan came over later in the evening and brought Katherine a gift. Jimmie was rather astounded at the sight of so many relatives.

"Every one has to be here," Katherine told him. "In all the wedding ceremonies, whenever a Deal is married, the question is asked, 'Do you solemnly promise to spend all your Christmases at Granny Deal's, forsaking all others as long as you shall live?' And if you can't promise,—out you go before you're in."

Abbie Deal was embarrassed beyond words. To speak so to a young man with whom you were keeping company!

Katherine went on, "No, sir,—it wouldn't be Christmas without the wax flowers in the parlor and the patent rocking-chair and the painting of the purple cow and the *whutnut*. Grandma makes us all animal cookies yet. Can you beat it? When I was big enough to read love stories by the dozens, she gave me 'The Frog That Would A-Wooing Go,'—not but that it had its romantic appeal, too. We always stay two nights and we have to have beds everywhere. Granny puts us in corners, on couches, sinks, bath-tubs, ironing-boards . . . and not one of us would miss it. Donald passed up a dance at the Fontanelle for it. You can't tell the reason, but the minute you see those old cedar trees and come up the lane under the Bombarded poplars with snow on 'em, you're just little and crazy over Christmas."

There were some very lovely presents the next morning,—the radio in its dull-finished cabinet for Abbie, jewelry, a fur, expensive toys and books,—an old musty smelling one for Emma, who had gone in for first and rare editions. Margaret gave her mother the painting of the prairie with the sunshine lying in little yellow-pink pools between the low rolling hills. "For I think you made me love it, Mother, when I was a little girl. I learned to see it through your eyes," she told her.

In the afternoon, Mackenzie Deal, the Omaha banker, in an overcoat and old muffler that had been his father's, spent a large share of his time out in the barn cracking walnuts on a cottonwood chunk. John Deal, the state legislator, went up into the hay-loft and potted a few pigeons with an old half-rusty gun. Isabelle Deal Rhodes, the well-known Chicago singer, called her husband to help her get the old reed-organ out of the storehouse. She dusted it, and then, amid a great deal of hilarity, pumped out, "By the Blue Alsatian Mountains." One of the keys gave forth no sound at all, so that whenever she came to it the young folks all shouted the missing note.

By evening the younger members of the group had gone,—Fred Jr. and his family back to Lincoln, Donald and Wentworth to Omaha, while Katherine was off somewhere with Jimmie

Buchanan. But the others, in the early dusk of the Christmas twilight, gathered in the parlor with the homely coal-burner and the lovely floor lamp, with Abbie's crude painting of the prairie and Margaret's exquisite one, with the what-not and the blue plush album and the tidy on the back of the patent-rocker.

"There was one Christmas we had, Mother," Mack said, "that I always remember more than the others. I can see the things yet,—my old brass cornet, a big wooden horse made out of logs, a tree that looked . . . well, I've never seen a tree since look so grand. Where in Sam Hill did you raise all the things in those days?"

"I think I know which one you mean," Abbie was reminiscent. "It was the year after the grass-hoppers. Well, my son, your father and I made all of those things out of sticks and rags and patches and love."

It brought on a flood of reminiscences.

"Remember, Mack, the Sunday afternoon we were herding hogs on the prairie and that Jake Smith who kept the store at Unadilla, came along with his girl in a spring wagon, and threw a whole handful of stick candy out in the grass for us?" Mrs. Frederick Hamilton Baker, well-known artist and club woman of Lincoln, was speaking.

"Do I? I can see them yet, red and white-striped,—and looking as big as barber-poles to me. I wondered how any one in the world could be that rich and lavish," Mackenzie Deal, a vice-president of one of the Omaha banks, was answering.

"And do you remember, John, how scared you were . . . the time we chased the calf and you grabbed it by the tail when it ran by you and the tail was frozen and came off in your hands?"

When they had all laughed at the recollection, Isabelle put in, "But I'll bet he wasn't as scared as I was once, . . . the time a man came to the door and told Father he was drawn on the jury. You all stood around looking solemn, and I took a run for Mother's old wardrobe and hid in behind the clothes and cried."

"Why . . . what did you think?" They were all asking.

"Well, I knew 'jury' had something to do with law and jails and penitentiaries. And I had heard of 'hung,' 'quartered' and *'drawn'* so the inference was that Father was going to be hung in the penitentiary."

"That's as bad as I was." It was John. "Remember that preacher who used to stop at our house, the one with the beard that looked as though it was made out of yellow rope?"

"Who could forget it? He tied it up like a horse's tail when he ate." They were all answering at once.

"The first time he stopped, he said to Mack, 'What's your name, son?' Mack said, 'Mackenzie.' 'And what's yours, little man?' he said to me. I was so scared I said 'Mackenzie,' too. Can you beat it? I'll bet there isn't a kid living to-day as bashful as that."

And so they went on, recalling their childhood days,—days of sunburn and days of chilblains, of made-over clothes and corn-bread meals, of trudging behind plows or picking up potatoes, of work that was interwoven with fun, because youth was youth. Prairie children never forget.

Far into the evening they sat around the old coal burner, talking and laughing, with tears not far behind the laughter,—the state legislator and the banker, the artist, the singer, and the college teacher. And in their midst, rocking and smiling, sat the little old lady who had brought them up with a song upon her lips and a lantern in her hand.

Low Lies His Bed

THE west-bound flyer was pulling into Parker City three days before—

Still, if one had been there it would not have been necessary to specify the time of year. Too many conspicuous characteristics of the period would have been about one; too many pointed allusions to it made by the passengers. Bunches of holly on the furs of four gay college girls, their eyes as bright and shining as the berries. The occasional swift rush of hard snowflakes against the car's double windows. All the racks overhead containing packages of grotesque shapes. The high strident voice of a child in the rear of the pullman: "But Mother, he couldn't get down *Elsie's* chimbly, *could* he, Mother?" The traveling man across the way: "Christmas trade picked up any, Bill?"

To old Mrs. David Daniel Parker, sitting stiffly on the plush seat, the sounds and sights of the holiday time came indistinctly, like little waves washing against a stone statue at the water's edge. Indifferent alike to the exuberant laughter of the young girls and the child's excited questioning and the results of any one's selling ability, she stared straight ahead, her eyes fixed rigidly on the blue velvet hat of the woman ahead of her, using the shininess of its cut-steel buckle as a sort of tangible object to which she might tie her rousing emotions.

They had been subdued of late years—those culprit feelings; had become far more obedient to her than the limbs of her frail old body. Joy. Sorrow. Love. Fear. Regret. She had known them intimately in her long years of life and been violently swayed by them all. But they had been held in check so long by an inflexible will that they were subdued now, too cowed to bother her often with their insistent tuggings— in the last years had become but memories.

And now that they were awakening and creeping stealthily through the chambers of her heart, she tried to tie them to the glimmer of a steel buckle in the seat ahead. A poor hitching post for winged Memory!

Old Mrs. Parker was thin, slender of shoulder, her faded old eyes palely brown behind her gold glasses. The snow-whiteness of her hair under her soft black hat made a scarcely perceptible line against the waxen hue of her face. Her coat was of finest seal and only a close observer would have noticed that the sleeves were short from having been turned in and the elbows showed long elliptical patches of skin.

She sat firmly erect, her black-gloved hands folded on an ebony cane. At her side were two worn bags embossed in scarred gold with D. D. P., their once-expensive leather covered with a dozen faded foreign labels. Another bag hanging limply from one of the crossed wrists was lettered in matching gold. Mrs. Parker knew that in the bag were a change of glasses, two neatly folded handkerchiefs, a purse containing four dollars and a rather important paper.

Although it was thirty-five years since she had been here, she knew by the swaying of the coach that they were passing around the bend now. That would be by the old picnic grounds, she thought, but she did not look out to verify her intuition—merely gazed stonily ahead, centering her attention on the shining buckle, as though she watched defiantly to see that Memory did not escape to annoy her.

Then suddenly, the train was stopping, and the buckle was leaving, and she became panicky, looking about her rather wildly. The porter came immediately, assisting her to her feet and taking the bags—the two worn bags of fine leather. But old Mrs. Parker kept the other in her hand—the one with the glasses and the handkerchiefs and the last four dollars of a half-million—and the rather important paper which was to admit her to the Old Ladies' Home.

It took her some time to get down the steps, the black gold-handled cane making the descent with tapping assistance. A man and a woman with beaming fat faces came to her through the crowd.

"I'm Mrs. McIntosh," the stout woman said —"the matron, you know. My husband—*Mr.* McIntosh, Mrs. Parker. And we're so *glad* to have you—and just at Christmas, too."

The stout man repeated the idea, echo-like, "Yes. Yes. And we're glad, indeed, to have you come at Christmas time."

Old Mrs. Parker had a brief moment in which she thought how very much alike the two looked. Their round fat faces slightly red-veined, their double chins, their prominent blue eyes, the very shape of their glasses were similar, as though they might have changed clothes and no one been the wiser.

They took her arms, one on each side like

symmetrical pillars of support, and began to assist her to a waiting car.

"I can walk alone, thank you," said old Mrs. Parker, tall and slim and erect. And tapped out her own support across the station platform.

In the car they heaped attentions upon her, raised a shade, tucked the robe about her, pressed a cushion upon her, with their warm hospitable parrot-like ways.

"You'll want the shade raised, won't you?"

"Yes, raise the shade for her."

It took both of them to complete every move and statement.

"Let's put the cushion at your back."

"Yes, the cushion!"

It irritated old Mrs. Parker, tall and slim and erect.

They drove through the business streets bustling with pre-Christmas activity, gay with their greens and their fat little trees, across a park and a residence district. The matron called her attention to the new court-house and the new post-office and a widened boulevard.

"And here's our lovely Home." The woman pointed ahead.

"Yes, that's the Home." The man nodded.

In one fleeting glance Mrs. Parker saw the

long two-storied building back of clumps of big trees, bare now in the pale wintry weather—and shivered slightly. Immediately she was calm, telling herself not to let it happen again.

They were almost into the driveway when the matron exclaimed, "Oh, Edward, how careless! Whatever was the matter with us? Why didn't we think to drive up Jefferson Avenue past Mrs. Parker's *own* old home where she used to live so long ago?"

"Well, I declare! That *was* careless—the big old house where she used to live." He brought the car to a standstill on the curve of the drive.

"No. Go on. We'll go another day. Mrs. Parker will want to have tea now and rest."

"Yes, tea and rest."

They were out now and in the warm lobby. Christmas was in here, too—long drapings of evergreen from wall brackets and bright red wreaths in the doorways and poinsettia plants on stands. Across the far end of the hall sauntered an old lady with flashing knitting needles and gay-colored wools tucked under her arm. Two others peeped surreptitiously from a near-by doorway. Old Mrs. Parker winced and closed her eyes briefly.

Then the matron had taken her up to the

second floor in a smoothly running elevator, had escorted her to Room Twenty, had shown her the bath and the ample closet, asked if she could help about the settling, explained the dinner hour, bustled about hospitably, rearranged a drape—was gone.

Old Mrs. David Daniel Parker stood leaning on her cane, unmoving, in the center of the room. And so life had come to this. She was an old woman, worn out physically, burned out emotionally.

The door to the hall was still open, and through it came the sounds of soft footfalls, low voices, a bit of music. She did not want to see any of the other—other old ladies! She did not want to see any one. Now or ever. If she could just stay here alone in this room—until the end. . . .

She walked over to the door to close it, noticing for the first time the printed slip fastened on its polished surface. With peering eyes she stepped closer to read it: "This room has been furnished through the courtesy of the Parker City Thursday Club."

Her own old club, the one she had helped organize, whose social meetings had usually been held in the ample rooms of her lovely home, in the city that had been named for her husband's people.

For a time she stood, unseeing, then closed the door, tapped back to the soft depths of a large chair and sat down heavily. She could faintly hear music again in the building, the muffled sound of the elevator stopping, old laughter down the hall. Hard snowflakes tapped sharply against the pane like so many grains of white sand. The branches of an elm outside the window rubbed together in crisp rhythm. The shadows of the December afternoon lengthened, while old Mrs. David Daniel Parker with staring eyes sat stoically in the big chair donated through the courtesy of the Parker City Thursday Club.

An insistent rapping on the door roused her, brought her back from that long bitter trip into the realm of Memory. With labored movement she pulled herself to her feet and went again to the door.

A short old woman stood in the hallway, smiling up at her with toothless greeting. "Velcome home, Mis' Parker."

"Thank you," said old Mrs. Parker stiffly.

"I guess you don't know me." The old woman's short fat body shook with silent merriment as she wagged her head in mirthful glee. Her face was as seamed as a relief map with its rivers. Her coarse gray hair was screwed into a doorknob twist and across her ample bosom a safety pin was nobly endeavoring to assist a row of buttons in their effort to hold the two sides of her blue print dress together.

"No, I do not know you." Old Mrs. Parker stood, tall and aloof and unsmiling.

"I'm Anna. Anna Kleinschmidt who used to vash for you." And she held out the hard old hand that had rubbed ten thousand shirts. "I thought I'd come and velcome you."

The soft blue-veined hand of Mrs. Parker took the red one. "Oh! I remember. How are you, Anna?" It was not unkind in tone, nor kind. Just a statement without emotion. A question with no interest.

"I'm goot, I t'ank you. So goot that I ain't got a vorry in the vorld. And who could be better dan dat?" She smiled her cavernous smile.

"You work here?"

"Oh, no!" Old Anna Kleinschmidt bridled a little. "I *live* here—all de time. Room Fourteen, and my own bat'tub." It was not necessary for Mrs. Parker to know that, largely, she kept her overshoes and umbrella in that useful adjunct.

"Oh, yes. I see." For her part, old Mrs. Parker was through with the interview. She did not feel arrogant toward old Anna, was in no way too haughty to hold conversation with her; but she did not want to talk to any one, queen or wash-woman. She wanted only to be left alone. Peace —it was all she asked.

But old Anna did not consider that the volunteer welcoming committee of one had ceased to function. "I earn all my money by myself to come here. All but one hundred dollars. And den my arm gif out. And who do you suppose hear of it and say I shall come at vonce viddout vaiting and gif the rest of the money himself?" She paused for dramatic effect. "Mr. T'eadore Harms!"

Yes. Theodore Harms would do that.

Mrs. Parker knew him well. He had been her Harry's chum, had spent many a long-gone night under her roof, had worked in her husband's bank, had gone away and made a fortune. And so he had paid part of old Anna's way at the Home? How could she tell old Anna that if Theodore Harms had not paid *all* of her own expenses she, Mrs. David Daniel Parker, must needs have gone to the county home instead?

But old Anna had more to ask: "And Mr. Parker died, didn't he? Tsk! Tsk!"

"Yes." Anna need not know that it was by his own hand.

"My man died, too. My Emil. You remember? So goot, so kind to me. Alvays collect my vash money. Sometime even carry home the clothes himself. Alvays say, 'Mamma, don't pump all dat vater now; vait till it stop storming.'" And still old Anna was not through: "And your son, you lost him, too—your Harry?"

"In the war."

"And your daughter, too?"

"Yes."

"Tsk. Tsk. Poor dear! Poor dear!"

But Mrs. Parker was turning away now. She could not stand more.

"Vell," old Anna had a parting word, "a merry Christmas to you. Ve vill velcome you gladly."

A merry Christmas indeed! When there was nothing more in life. Nothing but bitterness and blackness and emptiness.

In the two days that followed, old Mrs. Parker lived in the midst of Christmas commotion and planning, but the activity of it washed like waves unnoticed against the stone statue that was herself. Once from a north window she had caught a glimpse of the cupola of her own old home through the winter trees, and had pulled down the shade.

But in the late gray afternoon of Christmas Eve she had raised the shade, almost against her own volition. Irresistibly some unseen force had seemed to draw her to the window again. An early light turning on from a near-by building threw the cupola into relief, its outline as distinct as a child's paper-doll house. At that moment a light flashed on in the tower room, two of the windows just discernible through the trees.

Suddenly old Mrs. Parker had a great desire to go down there. For the first time since coming she wanted to look upon it, desired deeply to see it lighted this Christmas Eve, to torture her sick mind further with the sight. With self-inflicted bruises she wanted to add to the anguish of her heart.

She began planning, craftily, as only those who are mentally ill can scheme. She knew they would be assembling for the tree soon after dinner in the big reception room. It would be necessary for her to be at the dinner table, so that no one would suspect her unusual plan. If her wraps could be handy she might be able to get out in the confusion that would follow the dinner.

With painstaking deliberation she wrapped her soft black hat and a scarf inside her coat, turning the fur side inward so that the worn lining only was visible. Her galoshes she would wear to dinner. No one would notice them under the long black skirt and she could not risk taking the time to put them on at the last moment. She went down early in that zero half-hour just preceding the meal when all were tidying themselves for dinner, and deposited her bundle in a small coat closet near the side entrance. The excitement of what she was doing gave her the first real interest in life since she had come.

When the bell rang, the old ladies came from their rooms, some spryly, some feebly, but all childishly eager.

The dinner tables were sparkling and gay with greens. Poinsettias paraded proudly down the center of each, and there were cards of crusted snow-covered bells at the plates.

There were several tables in the large room. Old Mrs. David Daniel Parker, who had eaten at the tables of governors and senators, ship cap-

tains and millionaires, sat at the same one with
old Anna Kleinschmidt, who in her darkest
days sometimes had not eaten at all. There
were three others at that particular table besides the matron—an old Mrs. Tuttle, as little
and brown and twittery as a partridge; an old
Mrs. Murphy, large and solid and immobile,
as though, having found a resting place after
many weary years, she wanted only to experience the luxury of fixity; and an old Mrs.
Sargent with magenta cheeks, flamboyant earrings, unbelievably ink-black hair and a distinct
line of demarcation between the gay youthful-
ness of her face and the wrinkled column of her
neck, like a gay Marie Antoinette head on the
shoulders of Whistler's Mother.

Mrs. McIntosh pinned a sprig of holly on
each old lady, on the flat old silken chest of Mrs.
David Daniel Parker and on the mountainous
gingham one of old Anna Kleinschmidt, and on
all the others.

Old Anna sat next to Mrs. Parker and was
excited to the point of hilarity. She drank her
tea with gusto, smacked her lips over the soup,
was exuberant as a child that there was to be
chicken. It was as though she were having all
the good things of life at once, as though she

were experiencing enough food, warmth and light for the first time in her life.

"Oh, if Emil could see me now," she whispered to Mrs. Parker. "*Ach Himmel!* Eatin' oyster soup until I could bust."

It would have been exceedingly distasteful to Mrs. Parker in other days, but now she did not care one way or the other. She looked upon her neither with dislike nor liking; was merely callous to those about her.

The dinner was over. All the old ladies were moving toward the parlors, some with excited exclamations in anticipation of the pleasant evening to come. Mrs. Parker with her cane stood by the coat-closet door waiting until the last one should go in. It was old Mrs. Sargent, preening before a glass, giving her too-inky hair a pat into place, her too-showy earrings a loving touch.

The hall was empty now. Old Mrs. Parker slipped into her ancient seal coat and her soft black hat and stepped out upon the side porch. It was colder than she had thought when in the shelter of the warm house, so she buttoned the coat tightly, turning up the collar, and tied the scarf over her hat. Then she started slowly down the drive, tapping her way along with careful steps.

Now that she had left the drive of the Home and was out on the street, she realized there was greater familiarity about the little city than she had sensed in her ride up from the station. There was the old Rhodes place looking fairly natural behind the street lights, and the Kennards's house, though changed into a duplex, was still recognizable. They brought back vivid memories of social events in a day when society was composed of a definite membership.

Old Mrs. Parker, tall and erect, tapped as rapidly forward as her bad limb would allow. Two blocks down this way and one over to the east. She had lost sight of the cupola of her old home, which up to this moment had guided her like a beacon.

Suddenly at the end of the second block her knee buckled, and she stumbled and would have fallen if she had not been close to a low brick wall. She clung to the iron railing above the bricks for a time until she felt that she could go on. But the damage was done; the knee had been twisted and pained with every step. It was snowing and colder.

She was frightened now, and thought with longing of the restful security of Room Twenty. She must get back somehow. That block around the corner to her old home seemed suddenly too long a journey to be attempted. She wanted to cry with disappointment as though she were missing a definite engagement there, as though in reality the family expected her.

But some one was coming down the street, some one short and squat with duck-like waddling, a shawl over her head.

Old Mrs. Parker had never been so glad to see any one. She grasped the outstretched hand of old Anna as though it were a life belt.

Old Anna was merry with chuckles at the smartness of her own mind. "I miss you and I look in your room, and vhen I find your coat gone, I know shust vhere to go. I say, 'Anna, vhere in de whole vorld vould you like most to go on dis Christmas Eve?' 'Back home,' I say to myself. 'Vell, dat's vhere Mis' Parker go, too.'" She chuckled. "Come, now. I help you."

With her cane on one side and old Anna on the other, Mrs. Parker went on.

There it was—the wide porch and the white pillars familiar against the dark bricks. Lights shone in every room, and each pane held its Christmas wreath. Beyond the French windows a tree stood tall and proud and erect. Like old Mrs. David Daniel Parker. Several children

were dancing about near the shining thing, and occasionally the form of an older person came into sight.

And then a strange thing happened. To the woman standing there on the walk, clutching her cane and old Anna, the scene was so familiar that she herself became an integral part of it. Although her frail old body stood, tall and erect, in the snow and the cold, her spirit seemed to merge into the family group there in the high-ceilinged room. The sensation was sharply poignant, infinitely precious.

Suddenly something broke—ice that had long covered her heart—sweeping out on a wave of Memory. Instead of a bitterness, she felt only tenderness at the familiar sight. In place of cold-ness, warmth.

"Ain't it nice," old Anna was saying, "dat it shust go on and on—Christmas lights and Christ-mas trees and Christmas spirit? All over town, no matter who lives in 'em, de nice Christmas candles burn on. In yours; in mine. My old house across de tracks—I go over to see it dis afternoon. De folks got nine kids, and dey vas all hollerin' about Christmas and tyin' holly on de dog—same as mine used to do." Old Anna shook her fat sides. "Come, shall ve go home now?"

"Yes. I'm ready to go—home."

There was the slow snowy walk back to the Home, where for a moment they saw the matron open the door at the side porch, heard her say something about "letting in a bit of fresh air" and a familiar echo from farther in the hall. "Yes, a little fresh air."

They waited under the trees until the door closed and the bulky shadow was gone, then they mounted the wide steps and went into the cheery warmth of the building.

A great circle of chairs was being made about the tree and all the old ladies were seating themselves with girlish commotion. It seemed they were going to sing. The carolers had been there and sung and the radio had given forth much melody, but now the old ladies were going to make Christmas music of their own. To create! Ah, that was the thing that could stimulate.

"Here, Mrs. Parker." "Sit here, Mrs. Parker." She was still new enough to be given a preferential politeness.

So old Mrs. Parker, as tall and erect and proud as the Christmas tree, seated herself between the matron and old Mrs. Tuttle, who was as little and brown and fluttery as a partridge.

They took hold of hands to form a huge circle of arms around the tree.

"My, how cold your hand is," the matron said solicitously, "almost as though you'd been out-doors."

Old Anna Kleinschmidt leaned across old Mrs. Murphy. "It's the excitement and nervous-ness," she said to the matron, and as though she had just made a discovery: "*Ach Himmel!* Mine is, too. See?" And she put her hard old hand against the matron's cheek to prove her point, and then shook with noiseless laughter.

So with their hands—wrinkled old hands that had trimmed a thousand trees—they formed a circle around the cedar tree with its shining star at the top.

Old Mrs. Sargent, who had been a music teacher, gave the pitch, and the others joined in, their voices not quite in key, a bit cracked and hoarse, entirely aged—but energetic.

"Brightest and best of the sons of the morning!
  Shine on the darkness and lend us Thine aid:
  Star of the East, the horizon adorning . . ."

Surprisingly, old Mrs. Parker felt a lessening of bitterness, a lifting of shadows. Nothing was different. She was still here on the charity of Theodore Harms—not nearly so independent as old Anna, who had earned all but a hundred dollars; still sleeping on a bed furnished through the courtesy of the Thursday Club. But after all, she had lived a full life; with all these other old women had kindled Christmas fires on the hearthstone of a home.

"Cold on His cradle the dewdrops are shining,
    Low lies His bed with the beasts of the stall."

Yes, another had known anguish and sorrow and a lowly bed.

Old Mrs. Parker merely hummed the tune under her breath, but old Anna Kleinschmidt shouted it lustily:

"Angels adore Him in slumber reclining,
    Maker and Monarch who cares for us all!"

Another Brought Gifts

THE story of old Jed Miller is a story straight out of the horse and bugg—no, *cutter* days. It is as old-fashioned as the dripping tallow candles on Christmas trees in the eighties and as sentimental as a candy heart. The telling of it brings forth the memory of a combination of old odors: the delectable ones of molasses taffy and fresh popcorn balls; the pungent ones of Norway pine branches and burning wax; the stuffy one of the atmosphere in a small-town church on Christmas Eve. For Jed Miller and Christmas Eve were synonymous terms in those years.

Old Jed Miller was one of the humblest of the early inhabitants of that small inland town hewn there out of the forest on a midwestern river's bank. "Old Jed" every one had called him from his earliest days in the village, although he must have been rather young when he arrived with neither funds nor friends. Because of his weather-beaten countenance he looked old while he was still young; and because no deep worries or family responsibilities possessed him, he appeared not very much different when he had grown old. Old Jed Miller, the ageless!

He lived alone in a little unpainted house at the edge of the town back there in the days of its building. Maple Street ran up to the boundary line of his yard and then stopped suddenly, as though realizing there was little use to continue on past so unpretentious a place. Indeed, there had been little need for the street to come even that far, for Old Jed's callers were few—a fellow townsman to get him to cut cordwood; schoolboys wanting hickory sticks for some potential hockey game; an occasional book peddler, from whom Old Jed bought no book but whom he more than likely asked to stay and eat.

As the town grew and the cordwood was largely gone, with all the stumps in Main Street out of the way so that lumber wagons and high-topped buggies might safely roll along its dusty thoroughfare, Old Jed's occupation gradually changed. It grew to be that in the springtime women all over town waited for Jed to come and spade the lettuce beds or beat the carpets

thrown across the clotheslines in the prairie
wind.

In the midsummer, when the arguing with
various husbands over the weeds' growth in the
alleys brought no immediate results, the housewives sent determinedly for Jed to bring his
scythe and mow. In the fall, scarce a storm window went into place that was not guided by
Jed's calloused hands.

"I'm going to have Jed the first of the week,"
any woman might say.

"I've already spoken for him," another might
respond.

So Old Jed became as definitely town property
as the new waterworks' standpipe or the little
meadow which had been stylishly termed "the
park" since the building of the bandstand.

Although busy from the time the sun came
up behind the trees at the river's bend until it
slipped over the prairie's rim, Jed's weekly earn-
ings were small. A dime for this job, a quarter
for that one—whatever the women chose to pay
him—that was Jed's income. Because he could
have done nothing else well, they ·seemed to
think such modest jobs as the filling of a straw
bedtick or the planting of onion-sets should be
done almost gratuitously. But he managed to

get along in his own way and save a little toward that possible rainy day when the housewives might suddenly discontinue his services.

All this was on weekdays. Sunday was, as Jed himself might have expressed it, a horse of another stripe. On the Sabbath, Old Jed Miller dressed up and became a prominent citizen.

In the first of that early period, with the town but a new settlement and the church a modest frame, Jed's part in the Sunday services consisted in sitting behind the organ and pumping wind into the lungs of its cloth anatomy. His work was wholly voluntary. No one thought of paying him anything for it. In truth, in those days no one thought of paying anything for church work except the infinitesimal salary to the minister augmented by donations of coffee, sugar and molasses from the pound socials. If one had anything faintly approaching a singing voice, one donated one's musical output to the choir. If one could keep books in which exceedingly small sums of money were debited and credited, one occasionally and gratuitously became the treasurer. If one had a good flexible muscle in his right arm, as did Jed, one voluntarily turned cranks.

In time, because of the sticking of the old

organ's keys and the threatened collapse of a lung, when even Jed's muscular right arm could no longer coax wind into its asthmatic interior, it was put aside and a modest pipe organ installed.

With no questioning of church authorities and without benefit of appointment, at the first practice for dedication, Jed Miller with greased hair and in a new too-blue suit, arrived to disappear importantly behind a wing of the new organ and begin another decade of pumping.

When the organist took her seat and the Gloria rolled forth, a member of the choir who could see Jed from where she sat said that his face shone with the apparent joy of being an accessory to these melodious notes. Perhaps it did something to Jed. It may be that in his simplicity of thought he gave the woman at the keys very little credit for the music, felt that it was he alone who caused the notes to pour forth on wings of song—for from that time he voluntarily added much of the care of the organ and the entire church to his services.

All this constituted the whole life of the quiet little man—a mere uninteresting existence of one who knew neither deep sorrow nor tumultuous joy, who would never experience either the ice or the fire of living.

If once a week, for a time, he felt real happiness, it was a mere ripple of pleasure by the side of a great tidal wave of excitement that overwhelmed him once a year. This was the high point of Jed's existence. Toward this hour was all else pointed. For this one exultant moment did he live. Christmas Eve at the church!

In those years of the eighties and nineties Santa Claus was a single entity—an individual upon whom one could count specifically in regard to time and place. You heard his bells and he arrived through the side door of the church onto the pulpit, frostladen and breathless. He bade you farewell and disappeared through the same door. You heard his bells die away in the distance and knew he was gone for an interminable year. He did not walk the streets advertising toothpaste or barbecued sandwiches or basket-ball-games-in-the-Coliseum-several-good-seats-left-at-thirty-five-cents.

There was one and only one Santa. In that town he was Old Jed Miller, but of course you did not know that for many years. You went to the church on that night of nights clothed in several layers of flannels, a dress, coat, muffler, knitted hood, mittens and overshoes. Wedged between equally well-equipped adults, you rode with them in the cutter, your short feet not quite reaching the warm soapstone, your mouth and nose filled with snow-laden air and buffalo hairs.

Even as you turned the corner near the church you saw the lights shining through the colored-glass windows out over the snow and in a sickening sensation of fear wondered if you had missed one moment of the rapture. Although practically nothing could have tempted the fat old mare to budge from the spot, you had to wait while she was tethered to the rail between the hitching posts.

When, at last, over crunching snow you went up the steps, your muscles twitching, your mouth dry—almost were you ill in the pit of the stomach. At the doorway you gazed upon Paradise, with a swooning of senses at the sight. Resuscitated after that first shock, they became as acute as a bird dog's.

For the eyes there was a great Norway pine sparkling against the white of the wall, packages on and under it, the shining pipes of the new organ beside it reaching up into heaven. . . . For the ears, the rustling of papers or angels' wings, it was hard to tell which, and the voices of the congregation singing "Joy to the World".... For the nose, odors of cinnamon and peppermint, fresh popcorn and cooked molasses, crushed balsam and burning wax.

In due time there followed a program to which you did or did not personally contribute, depending largely on the timely question of whether you were in a state of health or had just passed (or were in due process of acquiring) mumps, measles, chicken-pox, whooping-cough, or the shingles. But whether or not you donated your services, the pieces spoken were practically all known to you, being largely a repetition of those that had been perpetrated the year before and many years before that. There was the perennial Notta-creatcher-wa-stir-ring-not-teven-a-mouse, and one which had been handed down from year to year but which you had never satis-factorily translated, sounding as it did like "Lattuce in they clabbered, lattuce in they say."

The program happily over, you saw Old Jed Miller go behind the pipe organ again, heard the music of an old hymn which all would sing, sensed on the verge of a nervous breakdown that after its seven verses it was finally dying away into silence. And then ...

A stillness vast and limitless save for a hysterical giggle or two! This was the moment supreme—this the one toward which all the other moments of all the hours of the year were directed—so vital that the illness came again in the pit of your stomach, and your arms and legs twitched in an ecstasy of emotion.

There were bells tinkling faintly and far away, then closer, bringing every tingling hair root to life. Fascinated, you could not take your eyes from the side door, so that when it shook a little, you shook too. He never missed. How could he time himself so definitely to the program's end?

The bells jangled now with mad, breath-taking closeness. The door opened. He bounced in merrily, short and rotund, with a round little—*you know,* the word you ought not say out loud —that shook like a bowlful of jelly. The children roared their welcome—all but you. You hid your face for a moment because of the world-shaking event that was taking place.

He called "Merry Christmas, children!" many times and said that Pikeville was one of the places he liked best of all to come. He told what a hard time he had getting here and how the reindeer were stamping outside, impatient for him to hurry. Then he sauntered over to the tree and said well, well, he guessed he'd better begin to call the names on the packages. Thereupon he handed them out with such intimate comments that it was unbelievable how he could know so much town gossip.

When you went up for yours he said something so personal that you realized anew how uncanny was his knowledge of your everyday life. Sometimes he called the boys by family nicknames which you would scarcely have expected him to know: "Tweet," or "Tubby" or "Babe," so that every one in the audience laughed.

Yes, he knew every one. "Here's somethin' fer Tommie Graham. Hi, Tommie, what's this I hear tell ag'in' ye—hitchin' on to the back of Schmidt's grocery cart? Hev you been?"

"Y-yes, sir."

"Ye won't no more?"

"No, sir."

The audience roared, and, red-eared, Tommie received his gift.

He knew all, heard all, saw all—this Santa who stopped here en route to other towns.

Sometimes, when the exercises were nearly over, a swaggering older youth whispered across to you: "Ho, ho! You think that's a real Santa Claus, don't you? Well, it ain't. It's Old Jed Miller dressed up thataway."

But questioned, your parents had the retort supreme for you. "Didn't you see Old Jed Miller go behind the organ to pump and never come out?"

It was true. You admitted the fact of seeing old man Miller disappear into the cavernous depths behind the organ, and because you were unaware that a panel in the sturdy oak wall slipped out of place if one knew where to locate its sensitive spot, you admitted readily enough that Santa Claus came in while old man Miller was still behind there. Sometimes they added still another proof: "Wasn't Santa Claus fat? And isn't old man Miller thin as a willow whistle?"

It silenced you, so that you were convinced for another year, and no hulking boy with bragging tongue could shake your faith.

The thing that gave you the most confidence in the fabulous wealth and generosity of the little man in red was the fact that when the gifts had all been handed out, he called the boys and girls to the platform—that is, all those who had not reached their tenth birthday. Unbelievably he gave each one money. Thirty, forty, fifty, even sixty boys and girls—he gave them all a shining quarter. He had done so for years.

He had one ruling. Every child must walk up to the tree by himself. No babies in arms and no holding parents' hands.

There were those who thought that Pikeville babies learned to walk earlier on account of the Santa Claus quarter.

It was traditional. All the presents given out, Santa walked to the edge of the platform and held up his hand for silence.... The older people in the audience laughed and nudged one another. "It's his big moment," and, "Just lives for it," you might hear, but not understand.

"Now I want all the boys 'n' girls who kin walk up here by theirselves—'n' is under ten—every one to come up ag'in." He patted the big pockets of his scarlet coat and called out in his commanding voice: "I've got a little somethin' else fer each one of you."

The rush to the Klondike then began.

Santa Claus held up his hand for silence. "I've watched all the children of this here town 'n' I sez to myself, sez I, they're pretty good young-uns; I guess I'll give every one some money."

There was lusty shouting, so that he held up

his hand again. If you were very close you saw
how worn and calloused it was, like a hand that
worked in gardens, and you wondered why.

"Before I go back to my home——"

("Where you live?" a bold boy perennially
asked. "Oh, up ayont Iceland er Greenland—
som'ers in *the Artics*.")

"——there's three things I want ye should
always remember. Live upright lives. Do some
good in the world with this here money I give
ye. And always keep the Christmas spirit in yer
hearts, and when ye git older, bring all the
happiness ye kin to other little children at
Christmas time. Do ye promise?"

"Oh, yes, sir."

"All right, then—here goes!"

Shining quarters—one for each child. Again
he knew about all the children. "Johnnie Quinn,
you got yer last one a year agone. You was ten in
July." Oh, my goodness, think of him knowing
that!

You clutched your quarter tightly and went
back to the pew where your parents sat grinning.
"Look, he gave me money."

"Well! Well!"

You clutched it all the way home—this different money that came from Iceland or **Green-**

land or *the Artics,* but was strangely the same kind of silver money your parents possessed on rare occasions. If you dropped it in the snow you bawled to the moon and held up the whole congregation on the steps until it was retrieved.

Santa had told you to do good with your money. Sometimes you gave it the very next Sunday to the Sunday school, so that you might rid yourself of all further responsibility in the ethics of its disposal. Sometimes, after due meditation in which you were torn between moral rectitude and the fleshpots, you sent it to the missionaries via the Ladies' Society with the righteous satisfaction of having converted countless heathens. Sometimes, human nature having been quite the same in the not-always-so-gay nineties, you bought huge white gum hearts and licorice with it, waiting conscience-smitten for bad luck to follow, immeasurably relieved when it failed to appear.

Always the little man ended with that same pronouncement which he gave like the benediction. "Remember! Live upright lives. Do something good with yer money. Always keep the Christmas spirit in yer hearts and try to make other children happy."

Ah, well, you were not always upright. You

did not always do good with your money. But, perhaps mellowed a little by that benediction of long ago, you did resurrect the Christmas spirit each year.

Then suddenly you were ten and had passed the traditional quarter-gift age—too soon knew the disillusioning truth. Santa Claus *was* old man Miller. It was disappointing, but after the shock of the discovery was over, you joined the conspirators. Because you had so loved the great moment, you, too, kept silent and saw the other little children of the town walk up excitedly for their money.

Then after a time, when you were much older, you saw something else: the drama and the pathos that were old man Miller. You saw how all year old Jed Miller lived for this one hour of giving. It seemed foolish, saving from his small wages to give it away in one reckless hour of abandon. Don Quixote mowing lawns! Pikeville called it plain dumb.

And then the old man grew feeble and rather forgetful but still he gave much of his time to the church, although it must have been harder for him. He annoyed some of the people, particularly the Reverend Julius Parkinson who had come from a larger place, for before the services Old Jed would squeak-squeak about the church, fussily passing out extra hymn-books, getting down on his knees to hunt for a child's lost penny.

The membership was changing. There were more important people in it now—Mrs. Adelbert Tobin, for instance, who was both a pillar and a power. She and the Reverend Parkinson agreed between them that the services would possess more dignity without the preliminary squeak-ings of Old Jed.

"He's an institution," a few old-timers pro-tested.

"He's a nuisance," Mrs. Tobin retorted.

So a new and younger man was asked to care for the church and surprisingly given a small wage for doing so.

You may tell an old family dog that he is no longer a member of the family but it means practically nothing to him. With this same pleas-ant scope of vision, Old Jed chose to look upon the newcomer as a mere assistant and went about his faithful, if squeaking, way.

And then, Christmas was coming. Mrs. Tobin was to have charge of the exercises and she ex-plained to Jed that they were dispensing with his services behind the organ and simultaneously with his Santa Claus impersonation.

"I won't have him spoiling my program with his crude ways and illiterate speech," she announced. "The time has come to tell him so in plain words."

There could be no mistaking the plainness of Mrs. Tobin's words. She told Jed they were to have a pageant this year—a beautiful, moving artistic pageant. There would be Joseph and Mary and the Christ Child, shepherds and wise men and angels. Children would represent Hope and Courage, Fear and Selfishness, Truth and Service, Love and Faith. In fact, every perfection and every frailty attendant upon humans was to be represented in Mrs. Tobin's artistic pageant; everything in short, except a fat Santa Claus in a disreputable old red suit and dirty white whiskers. She told the other ladies that she thought for once Old Jed had got it through his head.

And she was quite right. Old Jed got it through his head. All the life went out of him. He disappeared from church and from his old haunts. When it occurred to some one that he had not been seen around much, Doctor Waters went down to the unpainted house at the end of Maple Street. He found Old Jed in bed, told questioners uptown that he guessed the old man was about done for. He left him medicine, told him to keep quiet and promised to drop in again.

Christmas Eve came with the lights from the church streaming out on the snow and the Norway pine green and sparkling against the white wall.

Every one had to give Mrs. Tobin credit for her pageant. It *was* more artistic than the old "pieces" spoken in hodge-podge order. There was a nice dignity about the whole program with its aura of spiritual significance, as Mrs. Tobin had so aptly predicted. The wise men and the shepherds, Truth and Service, Hope and Love were letter-perfect. The angels sang their final song and the pageant was over, when bells sounded loudly at the side door. Mrs. Tobin looked startled, and every child drew in an excited breath.

The door opened and into the midst of the artistry and the spiritual significance bounced a little old Santa Claus in a disreputable red suit and dirty white whiskers. Every child let out its breath in one wild shout. Every parent said, "Of all things!" or, "Thought he was sick."

Doctor Waters half rose from his seat and sat

down again. Mrs. Tobin gave a very good imitation of a lady smiling when eating a lemon.

"Bet ye thought I might not git here, but here I be." He might have swayed a little.

The dignified pageant turned to a riot, noisy and hilarious. Santa gave out the presents, calling names with gusto and adding personal comments to every excited child who came for them.

" 'N' now I got somepin fer everybody here under ten." He slapped his heavy pockets. "I be'n watchin' the children o' this here town 'n' I sez they's pretty good. So I looks all around my house. . . ."

"Where is it?" called the perennially bold one.

"Oh, I ain't tellin'. Som'ers up ayont Iceland er Greenland—er *the Artics.*"

There was a quarter for each one, as there had been for over thirty years. It was just as the silver shower ended that it happened.

A little flame suddenly darted up from a dipping candle on the tree, curled its yellow-red tongue around the branch, leaped to the next one.

Women screamed. Men jumped to their feet. Children stood fascinated with horror, watching the little red tongues crackle toward the upper branches.

And then the little old Santa sprang to it, grasped the flaming thing in both arms, wrenched it from its sand-filled keg, and kicking open the side door, went out with his torchlike burden.

Doctor Waters hurried after the old man; a dozen adults followed.

They brought him in from the snow to the side room of the church. Doctor Waters said it was not the burns: that the old man should never have left his bed. "Must have been mighty hard for him to get dressed and come up here."

There was scarcely a dry eye there in the little room filled with grown people. It was not just that Old Jed was dying. It was the memory of those Christmas Eves when they had been little, so that it seemed Youth and Childish Happiness were going out with him now.

"The's three things." He roused himself, thinking they were children there around him. "Live upright lives. Do good with this here money. Always keep the Christmas spirit . . . 'n' make . . . other children happy. Do ye promise?"

"We promise."

Outside, people were grouped around the door. Children, clutching quarters, pestered their parents with questions. "What's happened to Santa? Did he get hurt?"

"No, nothing can happen to Santa."

"Well, who's that in there, then?"

"That's Old Jed Miller."

"Well, what's happened to *him?*"

"He's going away."

"Where?"

"Oh, up—maybe up beyond *the Artics.*"

Afterward, recalling how little work he had been able to do that year, every one realized how he must have skimped himself to save for that last Christmas.

Telling it after many years, the whole thing sounds too sentimental for this practical age. Such an outmoded tale about Old Jed Miller giving away his hard-earned money to the children—as old-fashioned as that one about the men who long ago brought Another Child gifts of gold and frankincense and myrrh.

Suzanne's Own Night

(From Song of Years)

CHRISTMAS EVE of 1855 in the Martins' big log-and-frame house there at the edge of the grove which swept up from the timberland along the Iowa's Red Cedar River!

It was very cold. Several settlers had frozen to death in near-by localities, so said the papers. There was a little newspaper in each town now, the *Iowa State Register* in Prairie Rapids, the *Banner* in Sturgis Falls. That was progress for you.

The west windows in the lean-to were packed solid with snow, the east ones only less so by a few square inches of peep-holes. The main room was warm as far as the fire from the four-foot logs could throw its heat. Beyond that it was as cold as though one stepped into another clime. In Sarah's bedroom the frost sparkled on the whitewashed logs of the walls. Up the loft ladders the east bedroom was only less cold than the out-doors by the slight advantage given from a roof breaking the sweep of prairie wind. The west loft had one mildly warm spot in it. By standing with one's back flattened against the wall where the fireplace chimney passed through, one could detect a faint response of heat.

But as standing with one's back flattened to a chimney was inconvenient for any protracted period, the inmates of the west chamber were as near to a state of freezing as those of the east. All the girls wore flannel nightgowns, flannel night-caps, and flannel bedsocks, and rather perilously, with much squealing, carried up the ladders each night pieces of hot soapstone wrapped in fragments of clean worn rugs. Safely up the ladders without having dropped hot stones on whoever came behind, they climbed onto feather-beds, pulled other feather-stuffed ticks and several pieced comforts over them, and if their clattering tongues ceased and their exuberant spirits calmed down sufficiently soon, were not long in going soundly to sleep.

To-night all were around the fireplace except Sabina, who was over in her Sturgis Falls home getting ready her first Christmas dinner for them all on the morrow. Henry and Lucy had come over from the other house so there were still eleven people. Lucy sat in Ma's red-covered rocker out of deference to her delicate condition, a concession that had its humorous side when one stopped to think that all year she had washed, ironed, baked, scrubbed, made soap, hoed in the garden, gone after the cows in the timber, and on occasion helped milk. But this was Christmas Eve and all at once every one was deferential to the Madonna-like potentialities of Lucy.

Christmas Eve was Suzanne's own night. It had been made for her. Sitting on the floor with her back to the edge of the fireplace, arms around her knees while the light played over the room, she had that feeling which always came with this special night. She could not put it into words which satisfied her, but in some vague way knew it was magic—the night for which one lived all year.

In the summer, with the mourning-doves and the bouncing-Bets, the wild grape-vine swings and the long walks in the timber, you forgot entirely the feeling that this night could bring. To think of it gave you no emotion whatever. In the early fall you began to remember it. By November it became a bright light toward which you walked. And now to-night you could not think with one bit of excitement how much you liked the summer things. Yes, it was magic. The snow piled against the window was not like other snows. The wind in the chimney was not like other winds. If you scratched a frosted place out of which to look, you saw that the snow-packed prairie to the north was a white country in which no other person lived, that the snow-packed timberland to the south was a white woods forever silent. It was as though there were no human at all in any direction but your own family. Christmas Eve was a white light that drew a magic circle around the members of your own family to hem them all in and fasten them together.

Every one was laughing and talking there in front of the fire where the long knitted stockings hung. Soon now they would all get up and go after the funny-shaped packages hidden in drawers and under beds and put them in the stockings. Suzanne had something for every one —a little pincushion fitted into a river shell for each girl, a fancy box for Ma, with tiny shells fastened thick on it with glue made from old Rosy's hoofs, handkerchiefs hemmed from an outgrown petticoat for Pa, Phineas, and Henry, a corn-cob doll for—she still felt undecided whether or not it would be quite nice to put a corn-cob doll in Lucy's stocking.

The pale yellow light from the tallow candles on the shelf and the brighter reddish light from the wood logs made all the faces stand out from the darkness behind them.

Something about the magic of this night made the folks seem queer and different, too. You could not tell why, but to-night every poor quality about them fell away and only the good ones remained—Pa's big certainty that his way was always right, Ma's scolding, Henry's stubborn quietness, Phineas' smart-Aleck ways, Emily's freckled homeliness, Jeanie's silly changeableness, Phoebe Lou's teasing, Melinda's rough tomboyishness, Celia's vanity. Her heart warmed to them all.

"I'll never think of those imaginary people again," she told herself. "I'll just stay by my own real folks."

Pa was telling about Christmastime back in England; things his grandfather had told him that had come down in the tales from there—about the piping and dancing, the carols and the maskers and the woodcocks cooked in gin. "My great-grandfather's family was landed gentry back in the mother country. Ma's ancestor hung the light in Old North Church when the British was comin'. Ma says her father told her the man was to hang one light if they come by land and two if they was comin' by sea. Both sides they bore arms for the country, faithful and loyal. You children don't never need to take a back seat for anybody. Just hold up your head and speak up all your lives. Both sides good landed-gentry blood runs in your veins and . . ."

If you listened above the din of the talking you could hear the wind in the chimney turn into music. Christmas Eve was a night of song that wrapped itself about you like a shawl. But it warmed more than your body. It warmed your heart . . . filled it, too, with melody that would last forever. Even though you grew up and found you could never quite bring back the magic feeling of this night, the melody would stay in your heart always—a song for all the years.

The Silent Stars Go By

THE woman turned her head monotonously
back and forth on the pillow in the restless
way of the very ill. Her arms swung out from
under the silken quilts with the regularity of a
swimmer and with equal regularity were covered by the white-gowned nurse at her side. Little inarticulate murmurs like the moaning of a
peevish child slipped from her lips.

They were the only sounds in the stillness of
the big house save the muffled steps of the
woman's husband pacing up and down the thick-
carpeted hall like a sentinel on duty. If children's
voices from below sometimes penetrated the
quiet room they were broken off suddenly,
hushed by an unseen authority.

Beyond the silken daintiness of the noiseless
room, great moist snowflakes fluttered lazily onto
the window sills and the wide expanse of dead
lawn. Only beyond the driveway with its retain-
ing rope stretched between stone posts at the
entrance was there activity—the sound of cars

moving up and down the avenue, the laughter of young people running up the steps of the church near by, Christmas greens in their arms.

The woman vaguely sensed it all—the unusual quiet, the tense atmosphere, the strange experience of being ill at the Christmas season. At times her mind was hazy, unmindful of its surroundings, off on some far-away journey of unreality. At other times it snapped into lucidity, became so keen that it saw pictures in detailed clarity, as though magnified by a huge glass.

It was then that she remembered how cruel Life had been to her. It had betrayed her. She who had so loved Life had watched it turn upon her, crushing her. Now she was ill. And she did not particularly care.

Restlessly her eyes roved to the picture of the Christus in its silver frame across the room. She had bought it in Rome—had liked the tender look of compassion in the eyes and the pleading attitude of the outstretched arms. That was the summer she and Neal. . . . Her mind grew hazy and she could not recall the incident of the buying. For several moments she slipped away weakly on some dim, wandering journey, while the snowflakes fell clammily on the sills and the young people laughed on the near-by church steps.

Then suddenly she was snatched back to that clarity of vision in which the events of the past year were mercilessly detailed.

The year had been one long nightmare domineered by a colossal giant that people called Depression, as though they spoke the name of a human being. At first she had tried to joke away this phantom of the times—to ignore it. But the Thing had developed a Machiavellian strength; had thrust its cruel, leering face upon them at every turn. There was the time when Neal had come home and said soberly, hesitatingly, "Janet, if the business should go ..."

She had laughed at that. Assuredly the business couldn't go—not the old House of Broderick founded in the early days of the state; not the wholesale firm established by the first old pioneer Broderick and carried on by his son and his son's son. Why, that business was as substantial as the good old soil and rocks upon which the great building stood.

But the business *had* gone. Nothing, apparently, could stop it—not the advance on Neal's life insurance, the mortgage on the home, the loans on real estate holdings, the Broderick farm, the sale of the summer cottage, her own money, invested since the days of her voice teaching—not all these, combined, could stay the oncoming of the hideous Thing.

Far into countless nights Neal had wrestled with the problem, but it had been time wasted. There was the dark day when he had come home and said it was all over. In that moment Life for her had been over, too. But if Life in its larger sense had ceased, mere existence had not. That went on—an animal-like state of being, in which one merely made an attempt to eat and sleep.

She had been obliged to drag on, even though the very house in which she now lay ill was no longer their own. The house she had planned with prideful forethought, had furnished with such taste that all their friends admired the beauty of it! She had no right to be here now in her own room. But she had been taken ill, and some one—whoever it was—must have been kind and told them to stay until she was well. *Kind!* Was there kindness in the world any more?

Involuntarily her eyes went to the Christ. Even He did not feel the compassion toward people He once felt. She was sure of that.

The nurse brought medicine and rearranged

a pillow. In a few moments the woman floated off again on dark waters and did not know where she was drifting.

After a time a bell, tapping at the church, roused her so that her mind snapped back again to its former acuteness and took up its ceaseless burden of thought.

Broderick's had failed. And failure was something she could not tolerate in a human. She ought not to blame Neal. He had been caught like a wild thing in a trap. He had twisted and turned and writhed, but the trap had been made of the impregnable steel of unforeseen conditions. Other men had hung on though, somehow, and now that things were righting themselves, they were saved. Neal should have done something more to prevent the crash.

But there was no use going over all that again. Everything was gone, everything worth while, the entire setting of their lives, all that gave them their position in the community. Slowly and painfully she called the roll of their former activities: Chamber of Commerce—Neal was a past president. The Musical Arts Club—she had long been a director. Country Club, Tuesday Dinner Club . . .

A young boy's voice called out suddenly from below stairs and was as suddenly hushed.

The children! That was the most bitter draft of all. To fail Michael and Dorothy! Michael, who would have been the fourth in line for the business! Dorothy, who would have been a débutante some day in the city's most exclusive circle! To have brought children into the world, and then to fail them!

Everything of importance had been taken from the children: Miss Proudet, the French governess; Spence, the dancing teacher; all the people who had been training them for the future. If the children could not have modern advantages, what was there left for them in life? Parents who could not give their children the benefits of cultural things in this day and age were complete failures.

Some dual part of her mentality reasoned for a moment that she herself had known but the common comforts of a plain home and had been both happy and successful. But that had been years ago and times had changed. Her children ought to know nothing of those old economies. But all her plans for them were ended now—travel, social background. She could not give them anything without money. Life was too cruel.

Out on that misty, unknown sea she drifted for a moment, and then came back to sharply defined realities. She remembered that day in which Neal had come home with news. He had seemed quite like himself, energetic, alert, a little gay for the first time. Courage and faith and hope had shone from his eyes. But she had seen them fade at her lack of elation. Carter and Price were opening a new department and they had come to him about taking charge. It was the first step toward rehabilitating himself, he had said.

Perhaps she should have been more pleased. But she had felt too bitter. Neal Broderick in another man's store, taking orders from other men! Of the various people in town who had experienced business reverses, none had fallen from such a height. There would be sneers and pity for the Brodericks. And she could stand the pity no better than the sneers.

Up to this time the rope stretched across the stone gates had been sufficient for keeping out disturbances. But it was failing now in its service. It could not successfully keep out the music. For, suddenly, from the old stone church on the corner a wave of melody came past the rope into the quiet of the sick room. The deep, resonant tones of the pipe-organ sent out the old song:

> O little town of Bethlehem!
> How still we see thee lie . . .

In through the open window, where the snow-flakes fluttered, it came with lovely cadence:

> Above thy deep and dreamless sleep
> The silent stars go by.

The nurse moved as if to close the window, remembered the doctor's orders for fresh air, and left it open.

The woman's music-loving soul groped toward the liquid notes of the melody as toward a light. The verses of the hymn were as distinct to her as though the organ were singing them. In reality she was merely sensing the words, having sung them so many times, but every syllable came clearly on the winter wind:

> Above thy deep and dreamless sleep
> The silent stars go by.

As her burdened heart felt the soothing message, her burning eyes sought the compassionate ones of the Christ and clung to them. In the haziness of her ill mind the thought of stars took possession of her, so that she felt no surprise when they began going past her, misty, brilliant, pale, large, with one of surpassing beauty in the distance. It hung quiveringly just above the Man holding out his arms with yearning compassion.

The stars seemed drowning her now, so that she gave a convulsive gasp and tried desperately to get her breath in the deep waves of light. She was vaguely conscious that the nurse was calling to some one beyond the doorway. The Christ became more faint. The music, too, grew fainter and far away.

> Above thy deep and dreamless sleep
> The silent stars go by.

She saw nothing now but the arms of the Christ held out to her. And suddenly the outstretched arms were no longer those of the Christ, but of her mother. She was vaguely surprised and happy.

"Do you remember—?" It was the old familiar voice, silenced now for a dozen years. "I promised to help you if you needed me. And I have come."

The woman felt a delicious sense of restfulness, a child-like faith that Mother would make everything all right. The sensation of lightness was as though a stone had been lifted from her heart. In her happiness she slipped out of bed and placed her hand in that of her mother. She had to look far up to the gentle face, as in her childhood days. It gave her such a feeling of childishness that when she glanced down again she was not greatly surprised to see that she had on a queer little plaid cloak with huge tin-looking buttons, and that her shoes were heavy and square-toed.

Hand in hand, the two went down the thickly carpeted hall and the wide stairway. No one paid any attention to their passing.

Only the silent stars went by.

At the outer door she hesitated, at a loss to know what was vaguely worrying her. Something hung over her, some forgotten duty held her back. It was queer that she felt both childish and maternal.

"The children," she explained to her waiting mother. "Michael and Dorothy. I must get them." She seemed to have a dual personality, to be both the child of her mother and the mother of her children.

"Of course; you must always look after the children."

So there was nothing incongruous in the children's coming from the library and completing the group, Michael in his jaunty suit and Dorothy in her tailored dress. And she in the funny plaid cloak with the tin-looking buttons.

Together the three went down the steps with the tall, gentle mother, and it was as if she were the mother of them all.

Nor was there anything so surprising about the fact that her father was waiting for them in a double-seated cutter, her brother and sister on the front seat with him. Her sturdy father helped them all in, clucked to the fat old horse, who moved off with a jangle of bells.

Down dark streets they rode on the crusted snow, sleigh bells ringing and children laughing.

> Yet in thy dark streets shineth
> The everlasting light.

It was Christmas Eve and the family was on its way to the church, the old breath-taking glamour over it all.

> The hopes and fears of all the years
> Are met in thee to-night.

She was filled with an almost delirious ecstasy. "Isn't it nice? Isn't it fun? Don't you love it?" She peered around into the faces of Michael and Dorothy.

She had a peculiar feeling of being a mediator to stand between the two groups—the old and the new—interpreting each to the other. She felt a sense of complete harmony with each, desiring tremendously that Michael and Dorothy should like her plain, substantial father and mother, wanting her father and mother, brother and sister to be pleased with Michael and Dorothy.

At the church there was that old childish delight in wax candles on the tall fir trees, the expectation of receiving a gift, the wonder of the music.

> For Christ is born of Mary,
> And gathered all above,
> While mortals sleep, the angels keep
> Their watch of wondering love.

There was a present for each, including a funny little doll with homemade dresses for Dorothy and a huge jack-knife for Michael. She felt apologetic toward them for the simplicity of the gifts, yet they seemed not to mind. And evidently they were liking her parents. For, before the exercises were over, Dorothy was sitting close to the tall mother, and Michael, next to her father, was looking up proudly into the strong, bearded face of the man, apparently for his approval.

They all rode home in the two-seated cutter behind the fat old horse, their hilarity intensified by the anticipation of hanging up their stockings. And home, not at all strangely, was that familiar old wing-and-ell house in which her own childhood had been spent. Again she held that wistful hope of wanting Michael and Dorothy not to dislike it, not to make fun of the plain old place.

But evidently they had no intention of so doing. They entered it with interest, looked inquisitively through all the comfortable rooms, explored the low-ceilinged upper floor and the garret with its accumulation of queer old things and even went down into the cellar, sniffing with pleasure at the agreeable odors of apples and potatoes in their bins.

Mother set out a lunch on the kitchen table and, with much laughter and chatter, the family perched around the homely old room while they ate the plain but delicious food, Michael and Dorothy entering happily into the fun.

And the silent stars went by.

In the days that followed, with incongruously rapid changes of time and season, they were all making garden, were out with their sleds, were having bonfires, were at picnics on the creek bank, roasting potatoes in ashes, fishing, hunting meadow larks' nests.

With growing surprise she saw how thoroughly Michael and Dorothy entered into the life, what a comrade her father was making of Michael, what devotion existed between her mother and Dorothy.

The family did everything together, as always. Their contacts embodied much of the heart, something of the soul. Life in its simplicity was rich and full.

And now she began to be troubled. Some vague sense of responsibility for Michael and Dorothy asserted itself; some obligation that, as she had brought them here, so must she return them. She felt a haunting realization of the fact that unless she acted quickly she might lose her way back. It shook her complacency, lessened her enjoyment of the irresponsible days. In this dawning of the sense of her duty to them she became more maternal than childish; was, suddenly, all mother.

She began urging them to return.

Dorothy was deep in the mysteries of her first baking of cookies under Mother's instruction, Michael in the intricacies of putting together a piece of machinery under Father's supervision.

"But I don't want to go back."

"Neither do I."

She became worried; did not know how to break the illusion. "But you must. This isn't your life."

They seemed stubborn, standing their ground with consistent refusals.

"I don't want to."

"I don't either."

"But *why* don't you want to?"

"I like it here. I like everything. Don't you, Mikey?"

"Sure, I do. I like it lots better than back there."

She was confused, not knowing what to do. She looked about for aid in deciding the troublous question. And looking so, she saw her mother smiling down at her.

"Dear!" Her mother spoke compassionately. "Don't you understand? It was the spirit of our old home—more than the things in it." Even as she spoke she was slipping away.

The woman tried to call out to her mother, but the gentle face grew faint and far away. Only her arms were still outstretched in loving benediction. And suddenly her face became the face in the picture at the foot of the bed, and her arms were the arms of the Christus.

The woman was vaguely conscious that people were bending over her, that the doctor had his fingers on her wrist. She was aware that he was saying very low, relief in his voice, "All right now."

Neal was there at the side of the bed. "Janet, you're better?" All the concern of a worried man was in his eyes, the love of a devoted one, the protection of a strong one.

Her heart went out to him in sympathy for all his troubled days. She wanted to touch his hair, to run her fingers over the graying spots on his temples, but she had no strength. She wanted to tell him something, too, but she could not think what it was. She wanted deeply that he should understand a very lovely thing. But she could not put into language that which was merely ethereal and gossamer-winged.

"The children—where are they?" she asked weakly.

"The children," Neal said hurriedly. "She wants the children."

It was relayed down the hall—from nurse to some one else—to another below. "She wants the children."

Michael and Dorothy came into the sick room with exaggerated tiptoeing, a little frightened. To the woman they looked so little yet, she felt a deep desire to care for them, to give them more of herself, to carry on the comradeship they had but recently known.

"What is it you want, Mother?"

"Are you better, Mother?"

She gave them a brief, wan smile and whispered: "We had a nice time—back there—didn't we?"

They looked up at their father in startled inquiry.

He slipped his arms around their shoulders. "Don't worry," he explained. "Her mind wandered a bit, I guess. She's better now."

The woman looked up at the three standing there in close contact. She must tell them all a wonderful thing—something about the big things of life; something about a little home they four were going to have—somewhere. She searched her mind weakly for the heart-warming experience she wanted to describe. But she could not shape it into definite form. All she could remember was that, always, *above one's deep and dreamless sleep the silent stars go by.*

I Remember

THIS is not a story nor a journey into Christmas only, but something of the writer's own background and childhood, a group of memories not necessarily related to each other. I shall recall them as one picks apples out of a basket, this one—and this one—and this—

Many incidents in our childhood we can remember clearly. Some we cannot recall in their entirety. The ending is lost out of memory or the beginning has faded from mind and only a remnant of the happening stands out in clarity. Why has the beginning faded or the ending grown dim? We do not know.

The earliest half memory that I retain is the picture of a porch at the end of a long grassy path with low bushes on each side. There are flowers by the high steps and vines over a lattice. I seem to have been hunting for the place and am running up the path breathlessly, frightened and tired. My mother comes toward me, and while no words of conversation remain in my mind, the memory of relief and safety, after having been lost, is very strong.

The picture is so plain and yet so disconnected with definite time or place that, during my mother's lifetime, I asked her if she could help me decipher the puzzle, for I had a desire to associate the memory with its actual locality. Once or twice we discussed it as gravely as though it had been of vital importance. Was it at Grandmother Anderson's? No, because the path at Grandmother's curved around the house and this was straight. Was it up at Aunt Kit's? It couldn't have been, because she had an open stretch of grass and this had bushes beside the path. Was it over at Uncle Tom's? No, because he had no porch with high steps and a lattice, only a stoop. Perhaps it was a dream. Decidedly not. Dreams are shadows beside this clear picture. And so it remains—a little half memory, with no beginning and no end.

I was born to middle-aged parents at the tag end of their big family. Because they had seven grown and nearly grown children—the three oldest in their twenties when I arrived in their midst—I probably held the world's record for the number of bosses over me. Certain rare advantages attend such an administration. With impunity one can always tell some inquisitive adult member of the family that certain other adult members have given their permission to do thus and so. It usually stops all further annoying questions and is a method which was frequently employed by me. So I lived my childhood among a host of older people, playing, reading, fancifying, singularly free from responsibility.

Our home in Cedar Falls, Iowa, was plain and comfortable. It had started out to be a white-painted, green-shuttered type of eastern wing-and-ell house, but in my time additional bedrooms had been built onto it and atop it, so that its design was no longer catalogued in any architectural book, its painting a practical gray and the bedrooms numbering seven.

It had tall glowing coal stoves and many glass lamps, china wash bowls and pitchers, center tables and high bureaus, and an organ, until that most wonderful of birthdays when draymen backed up and unloaded a piano, leaving me stunned with surprise.

The walnut furniture was sturdy and unmatched. But through the cushioned depths of its big worn chairs I have sunk into the apple orchard of the March sisters in *Little Women* and into Caddam Wood with Babbie and the Little Minister, so far away that it seemed nothing could call me back. Once my mother took away a half-read book, one of the few things she ever did which seem not sensible, for I mentally constructed the rest of the story with far more disastrous results by the change of authors.

On the floor of our home were flowered carpets which had to be taken up twice a year, laid out on the grass and beaten into limp subjection, then put down again over a layer of papers and fresh oat straw. Part of the family crawled along one side of the room and pulled and tacked, while others smoothed down the straw so the results would not be hilly in spots.

Out in the carriage shed there were a high-topped buggy and a cutter, and in the barn a fat lazy mare named Nancy, which my father thought too rambunctious for the womenfolks to drive.

The front yard and narrow side ones belonged to my green-fingered mother. In them she could revel in flowers to her heart's content. During the long summers, columbine, roses, peonies, bleeding hearts, snowballs, flowering almond crowded each other in jealous profusion, while the porch was smothered in her specialty: fuchsias. Neighbors brought sickly fuchsias to her, as one takes an ailing animal to the veterinarian. She kept the plant a few weeks, returning it to the owner in a state of convalescence, her diagnosis: "It just needed a little loving."

But the back yard was my father's domain. No town lot ever knew more intensive farming. If he were alive today and could look out of my study window to a back yard of grassy lawn, flowers, lilac hedge and juniper, none of which is edible, he would join the pessimists who think the country is going to the dogs. For in his back yard every inch of space was utilized by eatables which served the family from the first lettuce leaf until the last turnip was dug. Incidentally, no modern child with his out-of-season vegetables can know the pleasure of nibbling those first baby lettuce leaves in the spring, like a starved rabbit, or wryly tackling an acrid pie-plant stalk, after a winter of fats and proteins.

It seems unbelievable that so much could be contained neatly in one backyard: the garden, a barn, a carriage house, chickens and their yard, a shed for wood (cut to its even stove lengths), a coal shed, sidewalks, a cherry tree, a little plum thicket, gooseberry and currant bushes, a grape arbor and hammock, with long rows of white and purple grapevines following the two high board fences. There was even a playhouse which my father had built for me. It had a real window which went up and down, providing the weather was not too dry for it to stay up, or too damp for it to go up at all. Its *pièce de résistance* was a discarded sewing machine upon which one could pedal furiously, pretending long journeys over land and sea and air, as though some god of Mechanics were whispering of such trips to come in the adult future.

It was my world. The woodshed was a medieval castle on whose steep-pitched roof one could cling precariously while looking over far-flung possessions. On occasion, whole paper doll families lived in the currant bushes. The plum thicket and dark spaces under the grapevines were grottoes to be explored. The paths between the vegetables were streets inhabited on both sides by temperamental ladies whose gowns were beet red or onion green; and when one of my big sisters returned from a trip to New York, the widest lane suddenly became Fifth Avenue. A wish today for my little granddaughter would not be for more outside entertainment or material gifts from family and friends, but imagination and a stout and merry heart.

There were a great many relatives constantly coming and going, in and from our home: big brothers and their wives, big sisters and their husbands, uncles, aunts, cousins, second cousins, cousins by marriage, and those always welcome, if vaguely known, people designated by our parents as "early settlers we used to know." Constantly another plate was to be put on the table, an extra can of fruit brought from the cellar, more potatoes pared.

There was usually a good Danish girl to help, too, for a whole colony of Danes had come to town, fine people whose thrifty boys were to become merchants and bankers, and whose young girls were not then averse to working in kitchens. Our Hannah and our Lizetta stayed with us until their respective marriages. Once we had a Danish dentist, a smartly professional young woman, who wanted to "work out" while she learned good English, with everyone in the family joking about her choice of households, where the conversation was a bit careless, if sprightly.

Our parents had come into Iowa as pioneer settlers before their marriage, Mother at eighteen with her family, Father two years earlier with his own people, a cavalcade of wagons traveling out from Illinois, crossing the Mississippi on the ferry when there was not a railroad west of the river.

Mother drove one of her family's teams all the way out, and she used to tell about her wagon tipping over as she went up the steep bank of a creek bed, and how the eight precious sacks of flour tumbled into the water, and the goose feather pillows started floating down stream as though the geese had come alive, with all the young sisters hurrying along the bank after them and laughing so hard they could scarcely run.

Mother taught school for a time in a log building. Then she and Father were married on a New Year's Day in a log cabin from which the furniture had been moved to make room for the guests, a feasible procedure because the day was as balmy as spring. When the time for the ceremony arrived, Mother came down a ladder from the loft, but as though to offset this discrepancy, even if somewhat incongruous for her surroundings, she had a rather elaborate trousseau: a white wedding dress, a pink flowered silk, a gray silk plaid, and a long fringed white silk shawl and matching bonnet, purchased with her school money in Chicago and hauled out from Dubuque by team. That merchandise wagon, driven by my father, also brought her an iron-weight Seth Thomas clock and a high black walnut cupboard. The clock stands today in a niche expressly built for it in my own hall; and the cupboard is in my daughter's dining room, looking, for all its ninety-four years, a bit smug over the satiny hand polishing it recently received, and no doubt trying to forget that its dark doors were once my blackboard upon which many a "cat hat mat" have been chalk scribbled.

Father and Mother lived for years across the road from my Grandfather Streeter's farm. He died before I was born, but his personality had lived on, and I heard much about him on all sides. He was "the honorable Zimri Streeter," a member of the first Iowa legislature after the capitol was moved from Iowa City to the new Des Moines. He was known as "Old Blackhawk," representing as he did the county of that name, and also, because of his dry Yankee wit, "the Wag of the House." He had come into the

young state in 1852, no boy pioneering in the
virility of youth, but in his fifties, and with a
big family: his little wiry wife, three sons—of
whom my father was one—and seven daughters.
They were a sturdy long-lived people. One of
those daughters, when she was ninety-two, was
telling about the death of a sister. "Her doctor
wasn't any good," she confided. "She might have
lived years yet. Why, she was only eighty-six."

Because of the June freshets, the marshy land,
and the crossing of the swollen Wapsipinicon,
it took the wagons three weeks to travel that last
hundred miles from Dubuque on the Mississippi
to a point between the two clusters of cabins on
the Cedar River which became the cities of
Cedar Falls and Waterloo. There had not been
a house on the way excepting the log tavern at
Independence.

On dollar-and-a-quarter-per-acre government
land, they built their first cabin, and when the
report came that the Indians were on the war-
path all the settlers came hurrying to it because
the cabin was the largest, and because my grandfather had the leadership which some men natu-
rally possess. Old Zimri would tell them what
to do.

The scare went into nothing, as most of those

early Iowa scares did. A few were tragic, as the one near Lake Okoboji when all the white settlers were killed but the little Gardner girl, who saw her father shot, her mother and the other children clubbed to death, and whose daughter in time became my schoolmate.

Old Zimri was full of his jokes, and those seven daughters were as lively as jumping beans. I knew them only as middle-aged or old ladies, but because of their sprightliness then, can well believe how they overflowed the cabin with their merriment. They made their own clothes and their own fun, laughing their heads off at everything, with special hilarity for the tricks perpetrated on the young men courageous enough to come courting. So when, as a young girl, I read my first midwestern pioneer novel, I knew the author was not altogether right for picturing pioneer women as drab creatures forever standing forlornly at the doors of soddies or log cabins and quietly going mad. If my father's seven lively sisters had ever gone mad, at least it would not have been quietly.

Soon they began marrying the more hardy of the candidates who had borne up under the teasing. Mary took "the Justice;" Cornelia, the new doctor; Lavina, Lucinda and Julia, promising farmers. Lucy and Sarah married brothers. If you married one of the seven Streeter girls, you acquired a combustible sort of creature and an excellent cook. It would be noisy and argumentative in your home, but never monotonous. My father was their quiet brother. He had a mild drollery about him but was not very talkative. Those garrulous girls must have taken it out of him.

Both Grandfather's and Grandmother's roots reached deep into the New England of pre-Revolutionary days: back to Dr. John Streeter and a Stephan Streeter who married Ursula Adams, to Captain Remember Baker, one of the Green Mountain boys and a cousin of Ethan Allen, who was shot by an Indian, his head cut off, and buried by a British officer (a particularly gory and hair-raising episode to my childish ears).

Grandfather was one of the Iowa signers for the new Republican party when it split from the Whigs, and he may have been the first of the reactionaries, for there is an old letter from him, while the legislature was in session, in which he tells the family that he "probably did more setting on unwise measures than anyone in the House."

To say that he was politically minded is to put it far too mildly, for the story went that he would drop everything at the slightest provocation and go to town, there to argue over politics in the stores, on the street corners, or from the back of his disillusioned horse. Grandmother was serious and energetic, a worried little soul who wore a black lace cap in her older years. She had her own opinion of all this constant political harangue, and as he left for town was apt to call out to her liege lord: "Don't even *speak* to a Democrat today or you'll never get home."

Finally the Dubuque and Sioux City Railroad, later becoming the Illinois Central, came creeping across Grandfather's farm like a giant mole run, and the first train crossed his fields on April Fool's Day, 1861. But there the roadbed stopped, not to go on for four years. For a war was on.

Every life has its big moments, and Grandfather's came during the second Lincoln campaign. Governor Kirkwood appointed him to go down into Georgia, contact General Logan's Fifteenth Army Corps, and bring back the soldiers' votes. No, there wasn't any V-mail in 1864. He left with his flowered knapsack and arrived in Atlanta just as it fell. All communications to the North were cut and he was bottled up with the army and had to march with Sherman to the sea. Sixty-five years old then, he had to endure all the hardships of the march, subsisting at times on corn from the fields. But his only complaint when he got back was that he had lost his hat.

He idolized Lincoln, and on the day the news of the assassination came, in his grieving he went out alone into the timber and cut the initials A L in a tree, where they remained a half century, the rough bark growing in and filling the scars long before those other scars made by the fighting were healed.

Although he lived a long time after his great adventure, life must have been anticlimactic. Once he said to my mother: "Ever stop to think you can't do away with anything? Chop that maple down, burn the wood, and Ma'll up and leach the ashes for lye. Scatter the leaves and they'll make mulching. Seeds that have shook off will come up. No, sir, if you can't kill that old maple, you can't kill me. I'll be in something around here, even if it's the prairie grass or the wind in the timber."

He is in "something around here." A book.

My *Song Of Years*. And now the land he pre-empted a century ago is incorporated into a seventeen-hundred-acre airport. Planes drop down from the sky where only the wild geese flew, and land on runways built over the spot where his oxen and horses completed their five weeks journey out from Illinois.

It was several years before my birth that our parents had moved from the farm into that wing-and-ell house in Cedar Falls, one of Iowa's prettiest towns, set in the woods by the Cedar River.

A wandering Frenchman, one Gervais Paul Somaneaux, had found the lovely spot and built a cabin, then gone his light-footed way. A trapper lived around the stream for a time, but for eight years after his leaving no one trod its banks but red men. Then came two white settlers from Michigan and each built a cabin, to be followed by a group of brothers who bought their claims and water power. They built a sawmill and a gristmill, started a ferry and platted a village. In this manner were the Midwestern towns planted on the prairie grass or carved out of the forests.

Although our town was a half century old in

my childhood, there were still a few blocks of
native verdure into which little girls ventured
for only a few yards and scuttled back to the
safety of fences. But it had a homey, substantial
appearance and an educational atmosphere.
Public schools were among the best in the state.
There was an expanding normal school which
soon became a full-fledged college. There were
churches galore. Lodges and clubs were in full
swing. Hundreds of substantial homes, some
with many bay windows and gingerbread trimming, iron fences and hitching posts, clustered
along the maple-lined streets. There were local
band concerts and important lectures by famous
names, and the big event of college Commencement, which lasted three days and to which
whole families took lunch baskets and ate on
the green sloping campus. My first taste of
Shakespeare was the Commencement plays
given in a huge tent, and no Evans or Barrymore
or Olivier has thrilled me more than some lanky
college boy—attired in the velvet jacket of a professor's wife—under a slightly wilted Forest of
Arden, giving forth in good old Midwestern
twang: *"If there be truth in sight, you are my
Rosalind."*

There was bobsledding down Odell's Hill,

244 JOURNEY INTO CHRISTMAS

and there was the annual pilgrimage for wild
plums, red haws and thorn apples, although one
such journey culminated in painful lectures for
a small playmate and me because we came home
laden with fruits and flowers which looked
strangely domesticated to parental eyes. As my
fellow criminal became an English professor in
a state university, she must have shed any bad
effects of her one juvenile delinquency.

In our town there was camaraderie among all
the children. Danish Lutheran, German Evan-
gelical, Irish Catholic, two Jewesses—they were
all friends. The word "class" meant only what
grade you were in at school. "Our Town!" A
nice place in which to have spent one's childhood.

At least once each summer my parents took
me on a long and exciting trip. As the great day
approached, I lived in such a daze of anticipation that I was like the old woman in the nur-
sery rhyme: "Lauk a-mercy on me, this can't be
I." For we were going up to Mount Vernon
township to see my mother's people, and it was
nine miles away. And what length of time do
you think the trip would take us, jogging along
behind old Nancy? Just half as long as it recently

took a jet-propelled fighter plane to cross the continent. Lauk a-mercy on me, this *can't* be I.

With all those adults in the family, I was prepared for the journey by an assembly plant, belt line system: scrubbed by one big sister, combed by another, and buttoned by a third.

This sisterly triad saw us off in the high-topped buggy: my bewhiskered father, my gentle mother and excitable me. I had to sit on a stool between the two and so close to Nancy's hind quarters that every little while she would slap her coarse old tail across my face with all the effect of a hundred sharp fiddlestrings.

As we drove down the shady street, the town suddenly took on a different aspect than it held on ordinary days. By some legerdemain we had become sightseers, looking upon familiar scenes with the eyes of tourists. With the buggy whip Father would point out local historical spots as though I had never seen them before. "Soldiers getting ready to fight long ago, drilled there in the park with brooms and sticks over their shoulders." Or, "In the early days there used to be tree stumps right here in the middle of Main Street. Anybody got drunk, the town council would set them to grubbing out the stumps.

Folks said lots of mornings you could hear the axes going."

Above Nancy's clumping across the river bridge, he might call out: "See down there? About there's where we used to ford the river when we first came to Io*way*. Remember, Mother?" And in fatherly explanation to me: "Wasn't even any bridge across the Mississippi in 1852, let alone one here on the Cedar." Small wonder that his youthful passenger grew up to write Midwestern pioneer stories, when they were served practically with her food and drink.

Over "the dump" we went and out on the country road, narrow and grass-grown then, wide and paved now. At a certain point there were two ways to go, over the open road or the one at the edge of the woods. The treat was mine to choose, but instead of a treat, it became a torment, so fearful was I of missing something on the discarded one. I have since made the choice between going to New York or Hollywood with far less mental disturbance.

When the decision could be put off no longer: "Well . . . then . . . I guess . . . the woodsy way."

And soon there would be the woods road where the huge trees were so close together the sun scarcely penetrated, and the great shadows beyond concealed *no telling what.*

The ground was eternally damp with soggy leaves and uncountable timber flowers. There would be violets, Dutchmen's breeches, waxen Mayflowers, or the loveliest of them all, the bluebells. And at the side of the road itself, queer orange-colored lilies, wild sweet Williams, ox-eye daisies and thousands of shaggy, dusty-pink bouncing Bets. There were red-winged blackbirds, bobolinks, yellow-throated warblers, an occasional killdeer. Woodpeckers kept up their insistent knocking on tree doors which never opened to them. Brown thrashers whirled up from the grass. Meadow larks sang their hearts out on rail fences. Oh, many things one never sees from a speeding auto or cloud-topping plane.

Sometimes we happy three became so engrossed in the sights that Nancy would stop and snatch at the lush growth, and Father would let her nibble for a few moments as though she, too, must share in the pleasure of the day.

Finally we were turning into the farmyard where the big white house stood among the tall butternut trees. I remember it filled me with awe to think there had been another one just like it which burned down a few nights before the family was to move into it. I would close my eyes to picture the leaping flames and the black smoke, then open them hastily to the relief of seeing the sturdy house intact.

Butternuts dropped their dark green bombshells onto the dust of the driveway. Brown beehives followed the line of the picket fence toward the side door. The slanting cellar doors, covered with sunning milk crocks, were immaculate from sand scrubbing.

Father took old Nancy to the stable to be unhitched. When one made a call in the eighties and nineties, it lasted all day and included two full meals with a snack between. Uncle Jim, my mother's oldest brother, came up from the barn. He was short and heavy, with a broad, kind face and stubby beard. Aunt Sarah, whom he had married when he was an old bachelor of forty, came out, too. She was small and spry and wore her crow-black hair parted in stiff precision, combed down tightly over her ears like my china dolls.

Mother's easygoing relatives thought Aunt Sarah carried her neatness too far. She kept rag rugs over the carpets to protect them, and newspapers over the rag rugs to protect *them*. She

welcomed us hospitably, but before we went in
sent a sharp glance toward my stubby shoes to
see if they passed the acid test.

They tell us that memory is more related to
the sense of smell than to any of the others. It
must be true, for although the exact appearance
of the kitchen remains one of those half memories, I can still smell it—that combination of
homemade soap, freshly baked bread, cinnamon
rolls and the damp milky odor of the adjoining
buttery.

And now Aunt Sarah was saying: "Go right
on in. She's there in her room."

We went into the sunny east room. *And there
she was.*

My Grandmother Anderson sat in a big chair
with a hickory staff at her side and her full skirts
forming a gray calico pool around her. She was
in her eighties, short and dumpy, shaped like
the pictures of Queen Victoria. She wore a white
netting cap with wide strings tied under her
fat chin, and unlike Grandmother Streeter's
wrinkled and worried countenance beneath its
black cap, her face was placid and seemingly
without lines. She had no teeth and her soft lips
puckered into a little pink circle.

The first of the interview was always embarrassing to me and I seem to have required a bit of maternal pushing. She would then put her hands on top of my head, run stubby fingers into my hair, slip them down my face. "My . . . my!" she would say. "Hoo muckle hae ye grown." For my grandmother was Scotch and she was blind.

Because Mother always deferred to my grandmother's opinion, taught me by inference that she was someone practically perfect, she seemed the personification of Wisdom. She could tell about happenings in Scotland three-quarters of a century before. She could repeat whole psalms which she had memorized before the darkness overtook her. She knew who married whom in the Bible and their "begats." But more important to my expanding emotional side, she was Romance. I had heard the story many times.

As the young girl, Margaret, she had lived with her parents in their humble cottage on the Scottish moors. When she was sixteen a young man rode up one day and asked for water for his horse. He was from the gentry and had become separated from the rest of the hunting party. The two talked for a time and when he left, it was with the promise that he would come back to see her. This he did, many times, with the neighbors wagging their heads and saying no good would come of it. But young Basil loved the pretty Margaret, married her and took her to live with his mother in the large ancestral home. Grandmother would tell complacently that the first Sunday they went to church she refused to leave her parents to sit with the pew-paying gentry, so Basil went up to the loft with her.

Apparently Basil's mother was not too pleased with the little peasant daughter-in-law, but took her dutifully in hand to make a lady of her, dressing her differently and teaching her the duties of her new station in life. But when the girl grew too homesick, she would discard her finery and with her shawl over her head slip out to the stable for a saddle horse and ride across the moors to see her people.

In time Basil's mother died and Grandmother was sole mistress of the big house. Uncle Jim, Aunt Jane, Aunt Margaret and Aunt Isabelle were all born there. Aunt Jane especially remembered it well, for she was a girl of ten when they left it.

Basil took a trip to America to see what the new country was like, was gone for months, and there was a report that the vessel had been lost at sea. Previously he had signed notes for a friend, and when the creditors heard the ship was lost, they closed in on the estate to confiscate it. *Roup* signs were posted that the house and contents were to be sold. Because the horses could not be removed from the stable under the *roup* sign, Grandmother with two of the children walked over the moors to get her parents to come and bid on some of her personal belongings.

But the boat had not gone down. Grandfather arrived back in Liverpool, heard about his losses, and sent for the family to meet him there. They came, laden with as many possessions as had been saved from the sale, Grandmother carrying a basket containing her lovely Chelsea-ware china.

The journey to America was wild and perilous in the little sailing vessel, which was six weeks on the way. They went up the St. Lawrence, and at Quebec, two weeks later, my mother was born.

When they moved to the farming lands of Illinois, Grandmother's peasant blood asserted itself. Assisted by her oldest son, the dependable Uncle Jim, she became the real manager of the family, while Grandfather, fitted for no work, remained the white-shirted gentleman to the end, and died there. It was then that the family came on into Iowa by team and wagons, camping by the trail for the many weeks which the two-hundred-mile trip took.

All this story with its endless details fascinated me, and my grandmother became many things to my childish mind. She was Wisdom. She was Romance. She was Adventure. And through her, too, came a dawning realization of change. Before that mental expanding, life to me had been only today or at most the faraway time of next week or month. Now I sensed a longer period of slipping time, a remote past and a distant future. Grandmother had been slim and sparkling, pretty and sixteen. Here she sat, fat and toothless, blind and eighty-four. It was almost impossible to reconcile the two pictures. So came my first conception of life moving continuously on and with the moving, great changes taking place. It was very sad. At least it would have been, excepting for the fact that these summer reunions held no time for sadness.

Other relatives would arrive: Aunt Jane, Aunt Kit, Aunt Margaret and their husbands,

Uncle Rob and his wife, a miscellaneous assortment of cousins. There was a loaded table out under the butternut trees, with several chickens pecking about sociably near it in callous disregard of their fried friends on platters. Some of the cousins wielded long paper brushes over the table to frighten away the flies, a proceeding which seemed merely to annoy them slightly for they returned merrily to the feast.

Uncle Jim helped Grandmother out to the table and she came stepping along hesitantly, her staff tapping the ground. She lived on soft foods and while we were gorging on the chicken and sweet corn, she ate an egg upstanding in its wooden cup. I can even remember the way she tapped neatly around the top of the shell to remove it.

After dinner there was visiting under the trees and Uncle Rob tipped his chair against a tree, and in a clear voice sang "Mary Of The Wild Moor" and "Bonnie Charlie's Now Awa'." Mother's family could sit and visit pleasantly over inconsequentials longer than any group I have ever known. There was something about them which was very close knit. They were gentle and affectionate with each other, a bit too emotional maybe, and quite in contrast to my father's energetic, bantering people who were opinionated and spunky, covering their deepest emotions with flippant talk and joking feebly on their deathbeds.

But I know now that which no child understands at the time: *that there is something eminently satisfying and stabilizing in childhood to be surrounded by many relatives whose roots lie deep in a single community.* And should I not know? For I had sixteen sets of uncles and aunts who settled in and replenished that section of Iowa.

We had to leave early on account of the long trip home. It seems incredible that nine miles was ever thought such a journey. Grandmother took her hickory staff and followed us down the length of the picket fence, waving in our direction, as though she could see us drive away.

Back to our home on Franklin Street was back to another world far removed from the farm in Mount Vernon township, and brought with it a feeling of nothing to live for now that the big day was over, a depression of spirit, happily never lasting beyond the first "yoo hoo" from one of the neighborhood playmates.

And then, on a hot August day, we journeyed

back to Grandmother's house. Whether or not we drove by the woods or over the prairie road seemed immaterial on account of the strange thing they had told me. And although we chose the woodsy way again, everything was different. The bouncing Bets were wilted and pale. There was a noticeable lack of bird songs. Only the timber phoebe was calling plaintively, and the mourning dove.

At the farm the bees were buzzing, the crocks sunning on the cellar door, and the chickens pecking about unconcernedly. But a solemn hush was in the air and even the sunlight looked wan and queer. Horses and buggies were at the hitching posts and all the way down the fence. I had never seen a big black box like that before. It was out under the butternut trees in the very same place where she had sat so recently. Change again! *Things always change.*

The minister talked, and while I did not then comprehend his words I read them many years later in an old scrap book, and he had said: "Her life was filled with labors, *but was uneventful.*" Uneventful? To go from a peasant home to an aristocratic one, only to lose it later and go back to the soil for a living? To take the perilous six weeks voyage across the sea and to pioneer in the new Midwest? To make the trek by team to a still newer state, through prairie grass and creek bed and timberland? Something of that "uneventful life" is in *A Lantern In Her Hand.*

On that August afternoon the country choir sang, but not "Mary Of The Wild Moor" nor "Bonnie Charlie's Now Awa'," which I thought a grave error as they were her favorite songs.

We rode in a plodding line up the hill to the burying ground which Aunt Kit's husband had once given to the country community from his farm lands. Often we had to stop, and Nancy would try to snatch a morsel of greens, but Father jerked her up chidingly, as though today she must not do so pleasant a thing.

I remember the dusty grass and the 'hoppers getting up under my dress and leaving their tobacco stains on its whiteness, and the headstone of an aunt near by which said ISABELLE BELOVED WIFE. But most of all I remember my mother's tears, for she was not a crying woman. Standing by her side, my hand in hers, I had a sudden realization that the dead woman meant as much to my mother as my mother meant to me; that my mother's distress was as deep as mine would have been had she been lost to me. For the first time I knew what it was to feel more sorry for someone else than for myself. For the first time *I knew sympathy.*

We went back to the farm for a late afternoon meal under the trees. There was a feeling of relief in the air, with the usual good food and the relatives all visiting quietly together in their amiable way. Why, everything was going on as though nothing had happened! In childish self-questioning I could not understand it; with no philosophy to aid me, could not then accept the fact that life always closes over the vacancy and goes on.

They are memories of a vanished clan and an outmoded era, but for a time my grandmother was the center of both. As I write of them in my study, I can see in a corner cupboard beyond the fireplace, an ivory-colored cup and saucer with lavender blue flowers, the only one left from the Chelseaware set she carried so carefully on the journey from Scotland one hundred and thirteen years ago.

There are countless other memories of childhood:

Sunday school, with the circle of red painted chairs, and my singing lustily "Jesus Loves Even Me," but thinking for a long time it was Eve and me, that Adam's copartner and I were of special distinction.

The Easter egg hunt in my Sunday school teacher's home when I broke the blue vase and cried frightened tears, only to have her put an arm around me and say that no vase was worth a little girl's grief, for which I gave her a lifetime of admiration.

The day one of the numerous long-distance cousins came and her eagle eye lighting on me effacing myself under the table, dragging me forth with a sprightly "So this is the little cousin I've never seen" and sat down, pressing me close to her ample bosom and apparently forgetting me. To this day I can feel her smothering arms, see her plump hands clasped in front of my supine person and hear her voice going on above me while she married off or buried all the relatives. The misery in my eyes must have been lost on a mother and three big sisters, for they only assisted in the marrying and burying. That I didn't have the gumption to get myself out of the human trap is symbolic of the difference in the generations, for no modern child would stand it. My legs went to sleep and my brain atrophied. I used to think I sat there a month, but know now it couldn't have been more than a week.

Then there was public school, and the first visiting day for parents, with my mother coming and looking so nice in her black silk wrap and bonnet. But oh, the embarrassment of it! And I must never let her know how terrible she made me feel *because she came in the wrong door.*

And there was the matter of the paste. The teacher told us we were going to make scrap books, the very thought of it giving an added zest for living. Two girls were assigned to make flour paste at home and bring it for the whole room to use. I told my assembled family about the coming event, and one of the big sisters, sensing and sharing my happiness, said she would make me a jar of paste, too. When I bore it proudly to the teacher, as one contributing her share to society's welfare, she said shortly: "Well ... who told *you* to bring paste?" Crest-fallen, I took it to my desk, but Fate worked hand in hand with Retribution, for the two girls forgot theirs, and the teacher had to come down to my desk and ask for mine. A psychoanalyst would say it made its definite imprint, for more than once in adult life, when about to proffer some unasked favor, I have hesitated momentarily, wondering whether or not the "paste" would be well-received.

And in a higher grade there was the first experience in debating. The procedure was explained, including the new words "affirmative" and "negative." The question to be debated was: Resolved, that winter is better than summer. I was affirmative. And what's more, the *leader* of the affirmative. Came the great day and I went to the front of the room. "Ladies and gentlemen," I began, at which there was a faint titter proving that my appellation had been chosen unwisely. But I was firm with them. "Ladies and gentlemen," I repeated. "You can always get yourself warm on a cold winter day, but you *can't never* get yourself cool on a hot summer day." Maybe my earnest glibness caused the outburst, or maybe it was their pent-up emotion, but everyone broke into laughter. And the teacher said: "Sit down. This wasn't meant to be funny. If you can't think of good reasons, don't give any." I sat down. Funny? I had no more intention of being funny than Douglas did when he debated with Lincoln. Through all the years—at least until air conditioning became known—I have never changed my mind that you could always get yourself warm on a cold winter day but could never get yourself cool on a hot summer day.

The climax to childhood's long year was Christmas. In the summer it seemed too remote to visualize plainly or to feel its spirit deeply. It was a word, not an emotion. In the fall it began to take upon itself form and substance, like a light seen afar off. After Thanksgiving it was a steady glow toward which you walked with unwavering faith. A little later real preparations began: Packages were smuggled into the house. Absent members of the family came home. The table grew longer. The seven bedrooms filled up. Pies were made—cakes baked—cookies—candles — oysters — a tree — chickens — dressing—odors—mysteries— The radiance enveloped that child who was I like a mantle.

On Christmas Eve there was always an oyster supper, with dishes of crackers at strategic spots down the length of the table and bouquets of celery standing upright in their glass containers. After supper there was the trip to the church where the tree reached the rafters and you shared its brilliance with friends and neighbors. But even that was a mere forerunner of the excitement awaiting at home.

Everyone, from Father down, hung up his stocking. (Mine was no bobby-sox affair, but a long home-knitted one, as thick as a board and practically as stiff.) The scurrying about with the packages, long-hoarded, took until bedtime. Then the interval in which sleep would not come, and when it did arrive seemed surprisingly to have lasted only a few minutes before you were aroused by the shouting of the first "Merry Christmas" and realized that this was IT.

Dressing in the semidark with teeth chattering from excitement as much as from cold. Going downstairs to find a big breakfast of pancakes and sausages which you could scarcely eat because this was The Day. The table finally cleared of its cloth and everyone standing around its old walnut length. The waiting for some late comer, gone to bring the clothes baskets in which to throw the papers. Someone else saying to save the string. There was good stout cord on all those packages.

"All here, now?" No, someone was assembling the scissors.

"All ready now?"

"Yes . . . *now*." And life stood still, for its moment supreme had arrived.

With everyone watching, you went to your stocking under the old clock mantel and returned to the table with it. You were deliciously embarrassed with all those eyes upon you. On all sides people were making remarks which caused laughter. In all probability they did not remotely approach wit, but laughter comes easily to a happy child and you were happy. There was so much fun going on that in a sudden sweep of emotion you felt sorry for all the people all over town, all over the country, who could not live there in that rambling old house set high in its snowy yard.

That house has long been torn down and no one remembers what became of the old table. But younger families assemble around other tables, and sparks of the Christmas spirit from the old house rekindle the fires each year in homes from Long Island to Los Angeles.

There are countless other small childhood memories:

The constant runaways. To hear that thud ... thud ... thud ... coming nearer, with sound of splintering wood, and your heart pounding as loudly as the horse's hoofs while you ran up on a porch, "anybody's porch," as your parents had cautioned you to do.

Riding in a milk wagon one day with a 'teen-age brother while he stopped in front of houses and clanged his bell and the women came out with bowls into which he turned the milk from a quart measure, while germs—of which you had never heard—no doubt perched about on the bowls' brims.

Picnics at Rounds Bluffs, built up now with suburban homes, but deep timber then on a high bluff, below which ran the river, down to which the little boys always ran pell-mell im-mediately upon arriving, panting back again up the long steep incline. The eternal male forever showing off his prowess before the female of the species.

Many memories! Some clear and in their en-tirety. Others only half remembered, with the beginning lost or the ending forgotten. Some-day, surprisingly, we may be able to remember. For shall I not—on a day—go up a grassy path, afraid and tired, having been lost for a time? May not my mother come toward me, so that I experience a deep feeling of relief and safety? And quite suddenly I shall know the end of the story.   (₃)